CAN I KILL A FEW?

OF COURSE I CAN

VAIBHAV GUPTA

Contents

Foreword

- *"A gripping, thought-provoking roller coaster ride. A must-read for aficionados of detective work and spy tales." -Dr Ankur Gangal, Assistant Professor, NMIMS Indore Campus*

- *"Interesting, thrilling, and engaging – an amazing plot with captivating twists." -Dr. Gunjan Anand, Assistant Professor, Institute of Management, NIRMA University*

Preface

There's a saying: 'Do what you love in life.' But I often found myself as just another person caught in the rat race—studying hard, pursuing an MBA, planning for a job, and enjoying life on weekends, just like my parents wanted. Yet deep down, I always felt there should be something more, something that truly motivates me to enjoy life and not just go through the motions.

Although I discovered my passion for writing during my MBA, I realized that my love for creating things had existed since I was a kid. I would craft imaginary characters and dream up stories—it made me feel like I was doing something meaningful. Writing, for me, has become a journey of self-discovery.

This is my first story, and I started it without knowing much about writing. I just sat down to craft a sweet romantic tale, without knowing the ending. I let the words lead me, and guess what? Before I realized it, that romance had twisted into a crime thriller!

That's the magic of writing—the story takes on a life of its own.

WHO WAS THAT GIRL?

Robin

"Anne, laugh again, and I will throw you out of the car," I warned her.

"Robin," Anne continued to laugh, her eyes watering from the hilarity, "Look at your face! A twenty-nine-year-old, six-foot-tall guy gets slapped by a random girl."

"That wasn't my fault," I grumbled.

"Doesn't matter," she said, banging her legs in amusement. "Just imagine, a guy who never interacted much with girls gets slapped for kissing her neck."

"I told you, I lost my balance," I muttered.

"You lost balance?" Anne clutched her stomach from laughing so hard. "You weren't even drunk like me."

"Actually, yes, it was my mistake," I admitted, pushing the accelerator harder. "I should have refused to come to your friend's party. If I had not gone, none of this would have happened."

I was frustrated with my decision to go with Anne. A pang of guilt gripped my heart. Who was that girl? What must she be thinking of me right now? How was she feeling after our brief and rather embarrassing encounter? I had never intended to treat anyone, especially a girl, in such a manner.

The events of that unforgettable encounter replayed in my mind like a vivid dream. I was roaming around the hotel garden because it was boring inside, and everyone, including Anne and her friends, was busy drinking.

I saw a girl in the moonlight, seated on a bench. She exuded an enigmatic charm that left me breathless for a minute. A stark contrast to the light, typing something on her laptop, her black dress clinging to her curves, her long, wavy hair cascading over her shoulders—every detail of her seemed to etch itself into my memory.

My curious mind wanted a closer look at what she was doing here. As our gap decreased, my gaze was drawn to her earrings. She scented like a sweet, warm vanilla, filling my senses and intoxicating me with its lovely fragrance.

But that moment was embarrassing. Engulfed in the memory of that captivating encounter, my legs got stuck with something that made me unbalanced. As if on their own accord, my hands went over her shoulder, and my lips grazed her neck. This shook her up. Her laptop fell, she turned back away from me, and with an expression of a mix of feelings, I received a tight slap. My glasses went far away.

I was stunned by what happened suddenly and before I could clear things, she shouted, "Who the hell are you, idiot?"

"I..."

"Just shut up. Utter a word and you will die. Don't dare to move," she commanded, grabbing her laptop, and stepping away. I tried to follow, but she shot a warning glance over me.

"Don't move," she repeated, disappearing into the night. I was stunned and stood there till I lost sight of her.

The party was winding down, and guests slowly filtering out. I needed answers, so I returned to find Anne, but she was too drunk to help. Frustrated, I approached the receptionist, hoping she might have some information about the girl. But I was unable to tell her about that girl. Meanwhile, the girl had vanished, leaving no trace of her. An uneasy feeling settled over me as I wondered why she had left so abruptly. Why had not she reported me?

Left with no other options, I made my way home, my mind filled with unanswered questions. When I recounted the events to Anne, she only laughed, offering no help at all. I dropped her off and finally made my way to my home, collapsing into bed, the thoughts of this interaction running in my mind like a broken record.

The next morning, I dawned with memories of the previous night swirling in my mind, a tumultuous mix of guilt, attraction, embarrassment and an overwhelming desire to seek out that girl once. With a sense of determination, I made my way to my office headquarters, consumed with her thoughts.

Then, a flicker of memory sparked within me – the sight of airport tickets nestled on her laptop screen, revealing her imminent departure from Boston to New York. Her name was Emily, and without hesitation, I booked a ticket for the same flight, determined to confront her and make amends for our tumultuous encounter.

With the assistance of my connections, I secured a seat just beside Emily, waiting to meet her again but I felt nervous, unsure of how she would react to my presence.

Emily

The sunset streamed through the airport terminal windows, bathing the travellers warmly as they rushed to their gates. I readied myself for my flight to New York, still unsettled by the previous night's events.

As I made my way down the plane, my mind buzzed with thoughts of the previous night, the memory of that encounter with that idiot still fresh in my thoughts. Why do people drink if they can't hold it?

"Ma'am, your seat number is?" I showed my seat number to the cabin crew.

"This way Ma'am." I followed her hand looking towards my seat, lovely, it was a window one.

"Excuse me, Sir, can you give me a side, my seat is next to you," I asked a young man who was reading the newspaper like older people, his face was covered. He did not respond but gave me space to enter, I thought it was quite disrespectful, but anyways, I took my seat.

I got a glance at that mysterious person and I did not like his personality, a black-shirted man wearing an expensive Rado watch, and premium Gucci shoes, the proper persona of a rich brat, but anyway, I got my seat, I had to enjoy the view, I adjusted myself, viewed a little flying manual, bored from which I looked around the passengers, he was still holding newspaper like a statue. I was wondering if he was reading it or not. Finally, after fifteen minutes, the captain announced to fly. I was relaxed and looking outside for the take-off.

"Hey Emily, I am Robin" I heard someone calling my name, it was that newspaper guy, I turned around to look as he removed the paper.

What the hell, "What are you doing here?" He dared to introduce himself with a smile. Shock coursed through my veins, a jolt of adrenaline spiking as I struggled to process his sudden appearance.

"And how did you know my name, are you stalking me, look, stay away from me." Hearing my voice, the flight attendant intervened.

"What happened ma'am?"

"I want to change my seat; I don't want to sit with him." I want to get rid of him, I want him to get out of my sight.

"Sorry for the inconvenience ma'am, but since the flight just started and all the seats are filled you have to wait a few minutes, as we have to ask other passengers." her voice was gentle yet firm as she insisted that I remain seated for the time being.

Trapped in my seat, I had to endure him, when he smiled, I wished I could slap him again, my mind swirling with conflicting emotions. The memory of our last interaction replayed in my mind like a broken record, the sting of his touch still lingering on my skin. I could not shake the unease that settled over me. "What did you want from me?"

"Please relax Emily, I know what you are feeling right now, but give me a minute to explain." He requested gently.

"What is there to listen to now, you drunk man? Have you guys found a new way of disturbing girls?"

"No, no, no, I was not drunk! I have never been drunk in my life, I swear. Just trust me and give me a minute to explain what happened." Without much choice, I stared at him angrily and nodded.

His explanation for that sudden unbalanced movement was hard to accept, but seeing his genuine guilt eased my mind. It allowed me to release the lingering frustration from the previous night. I nodded as he spoke, feeling grateful for his honesty and understanding.

"But how did you know about my name?" "I saw that on your laptop screen."

"Hmm, nice observation." What the hell, he saw my name within a fraction of a second.

"I have to wonder, why did not you make a fuss about me and just slip away from the party?" he inquired folding the newspaper.

"I have already tangled myself with enough work lately, and I did not want to dive into another mess," I replied frankly.

"Oh, I see," he adjusted his shirt sleeves, tracing the veins and muscles of his hands.

The tension that had hung in the air between Robin and me seemed to dissipate, replaced by a tentative calmness as we exchanged further explanations and our conversation shifted to lighter topics.

"Ma'am, you can shift to B2, the sir there is ready to swap the seats." Shit, I got dismayed by the look of the flight attendant.

"Sorry ma'am but I am fine now, I want to sit here only."

"Oh, ok fine ma'am." She left with a look, might be thinking hell about me, but anyway.

"So, Robin, what brings you to New York? Business work or you like travelling?" I intrigued.

"Ahh, I boarded this plane to clear things up with you," he replied, surprising me with his candidness.

"Really?" I could not hide my astonishment. He left his work just to meet me and clear things out.

"But how did you know about my travel plans?"

"Again, I saw the ticket details on the screen of your laptop," he explained, and I somewhere impressed by his attention to detail.

"So, what's next for you?" he asked, his brown eyes seeming to sparkle under his glasses in the sunlight.

I hesitated earlier but it was a reflex and I shared my plans with him to visit my cousin in the city for a couple of days before returning home. It was a trip I had been looking forward to, a chance to reconnect with my cousin and take a break from the hustle and bustle of everyday life.

"What about you, what will you do now?" "Maybe I meet some of my friends there" "Oh, nice."

"So, when do you head back?" Robin asked, unfastening his seatbelt to settle more comfortably into his seat.

My return flight details slipped out in a flow.

"Well, why don't I hop on the same flight then? It would be nice to have some good company on the way back," he suggested with a smile, but I wonder if is it ok to be that close to a stranger. But his conviction and smile made me comfortable to say yes.

"So, what do you do, Robin?" I inquired, leaning in with genuine curiosity.

Robin leaned back, a playful glint in his eyes. "I am a senior manager at Clarified Vision, a marketing consulting firm based in Boston," he replied, my eyes met his Jawline.

"Oh, good." Was he lying to me, do marketing people have that much money as Robin carried in his persona, can they take a leave anytime they want to? I mused.

"What about you?"

"I am an ethical hacker, working for Techko Solutions, headquartered in Boston,"

"Wait a minute, let me save my bank details from you. Would not want any unexpected transactions popping up later," he quipped, quite a lame joke but his delivery was cute and forced me to join him in laughing.

"I don't even have your number," I admitted with a laugh, noticing the slight turbulence causing the cabin to sway gently, and I flung myself so close to him for a second that I felt his breath.

"Maybe you should have it," he suggested in a low voice.

"Well, that's one way to ask for a number," I moved back and with a laugh, we effortlessly exchanged numbers.

"We're almost there," Robin remarked, his voice tinged with a hint of excitement as he leaned closer to the window. The city lights twinkled like a sea of stars against the darkness of the night.

As I made my way through the bustling streets of New York City, my mind buzzed with thoughts of the intriguing man I had met on the flight. Robin's presence lingered in my thoughts, his brown eyes and easy smile leaving an indelible impression on my mind.

But as I navigated the crowded sidewalks, a nagging curiosity tugged at the corners of my mind. I could not shake the feeling that there was more to Robin than met the eye, a sense of mystery that intrigued me. Like a man who just boarded a plane to meet me and sort things out?

With a sense of determination, I went to my cousin's apartment and settled in with my laptop, the glow of the screen illuminating the dimly lit room. As an ethical hacker, I was no stranger to navigating the depths of the internet in search of information.

I began to search for any trace of Robin's presence online. To my surprise, I stumbled upon some details about his past experiences and his company. He is a man with a rich and varied history.

CHAPTER TWO

THE UNWANTED MESSAGE

Robin

As the plane touched down in New York City, my mind buzzed with a whirlwind of thoughts and emotions. Emily's presence had left an enjoyable impression on me, her laughter echoing in my mind long after the flight had ended.

There was something undeniably attractive about her, something that drew me in with an irresistible pull. From the way she smiled to the twinkle in her eyes, there was a warmth to her personality that was impossible to ignore.

The complexities of her character. Her athletic hourglass figure radiates an aura of confidence and self-assurance. I was captivated by the way her black dress hugged her curves in all the right places. And that one leg that slipped out through the slit in the fabric was enough to send my pulse racing with desire. But a nagging sense of unease lingered in my mind. I had lied to her about my profession as an undercover agent, a necessity in my line of work.

I got the message from the office that she had searched for me online. Thankfully, my carefully crafted online persona as a senior marketing manager would hold up under scrutiny. While Emily undoubtedly possesses impressive hacking skills, our hackers work tirelessly to maintain our fake personas.

I made no delay in booking the same return tickets as mentioned by Emily. An inexplicable desire coursed through my veins at the thought of spending more time with her.

There she was, radiant in her red outfit. "Hey," I greeted with a wave, feeling a flutter in my chest as she approached.

"Hey, how are you?"

"Great," we shook hands and moved towards our seats.

"So, how was your holiday?" I asked her, my face was brimming with enthusiasm.

"My holiday, oh you know what..." She recounted in a lively monologue about her holiday adventures and regaled me with tales of her extensive shopping spree, detailing no less than five shades of red dresses she had acquired. I was like what the hell, red is not red, it has varieties.

She eagerly displayed her latest nail art creations, proudly showing off her newly adorned nails. While I appreciated her excitement, I found myself both bemused and entertained, seriously if it were anyone else in her place, I might have been tempted to jump off the plane.

Thankfully, she got a break when the crew arrived with food. During that whole flight duration, I had listen to her quietly. Despite finding her storytelling somewhat dull, I feel a twinge of happiness at the glimpse into the life she had shared with me with that innocence.

"So, what's your plan now?" I asked while carrying the luggage.

Emily shrugged, a playful smile tugging at the corners of her lips. "Just book a cab, head home, and relax a little," I was a little upset at that moment as I wanted to spend a little more time with her.

"It is too late; I can drop you."

"Oh, no worries it is fine, the cab is on the way."

"You think you can get a cab in such a huge rush of people?"

"Oh, I have already booked one, it will be here soon." I was speechless, not wanting to make her feel forced or uncomfortable by asking again. So, I waited.

After a few minutes, a white colour sedan arrived with very old tyres, I could see the tread wear indicators flushed with the tread surface. I saw the opportunity. When the driver and Emily were busy loading the luggage at the back.

I made a quick sharp cut at the bottom of the tyre from the sharp side of my shoe and an explosive sound came out.

"Young man, I think you haven't checked your car for a long time, it got punctured due to luggage loading." The driver was shocked.

"But, how can it be possible, from the past several months I was riding it, it never happened before?"

"Maybe today was the day." I waited for Emily's reaction. "Oh, now what, how much time will it take to repair?" "Ma'am I don't have a stepney, it will take hours."

"Shit, what should I do now, all cabs are pre-booked and having a long wait." Here came my turn.

"Don't worry Emily, I can drop you."

"But..." She took a pause, "where are you going?" she asked, concerned she might be wasting my time.

"Where do you want to go?" "South End."

"Oh, what to worry about then, very near to Seaport Square."

At first, she hesitated, but I reassured her with a smile. "Come on, friend," I urged teasingly. "We can have a chat about more of your shopping stuff."

She rolled her eyes, but a soft laugh escaped her lips. "Oh, shut up, did I say much" she said, looking a little embarrassed.

"No way Emily, I like the enthusiasm with which you share things with me." With a shared laugh we headed towards my Porsche.

"Young man, can you please help us to load the luggage?" He was a nice guy and agreed without hesitation. I opened the door for Emily meanwhile that young man helped to load the luggage. Without letting in the notice of Emily, I went to that young man.

"Excuse me," he was looking a little tense.

"Take this and make the required repair for your car." I handed him two thousand dollars for the pain he had to incur. He went happily.

My mission was accomplished, and I headed towards the driving seat, Emily's red outfit was a perfect complement to the car's bold exterior. I activated the convertible roof to feel the fresh air just before sunrise, crisp and cool, carrying with it the promise of a new day.

My attention kept drifting back to Emily. I could see the curve of Emily's jawline and the softness of her lips. Her legs, her eyes, and the way her hair danced in the wind made my heart skip a beat.

We were sharing a peaceful quiet moment, lulled by the slow songs. Emily's voice broke the tranquillity. "Oh, I have been so caught up in recounting my day that I forgot to ask about yours. How was your holiday?" her question posed with a pang of guilt.

"Oh, unexpectedly, it was great," I replied, feeling a hint of amusement. "Anne is a free spirit, she also went to New York for some reason, though our thoughts don't always align, our vibes are next level."

"Anne, your girlfriend, umm-hmm?" her tone held a hint of curiosity.

I noticed a slight change in her expression. "Oh no, no, she's my colleague and a good friend," I clarified with a chuckle. "I call her 'walking bull' because she is never afraid to speak her mind. She is the kind of person who can turn a five-minute topic into a two-hour conversation. Tough as nails and fearless when it comes to standing up for herself."

A hint of curiosity danced in Emily's eyes, tinged with a subtle shade of jealousy. "Oh, wow. I would love to meet this one-of-a-kind girl," she remarked, briefly glancing at her phone before returning her gaze to mine.

"I have to warn you, though—once she starts, there's no stopping her," I cautioned with a grin. "She's a master at the art of roasting."

"Sounds like my kind of challenge," Emily replied, a mischievous sparkle in her eyes, and we shared a laugh.

Everything was going smoothly until I read Anne's message, a wave of tension washed over me, disrupting the calm of the moment. I quickly glanced at the notification, trying to mask the sudden unease that gripped me.

Emily's concerned voice broke through my thoughts, bringing me back to the present. "Are you alright, Robin? You seem a bit off suddenly," she inquired, her eyes searching mine.

"Just a slight headache from the journey, nothing serious," I reassured her, wiping away a bead of sweat.

"Okay, if you say so. But how about we grab a coffee? It might help," Emily suggested, her optimism shining through despite the underlying tension. "And the sunset from my balcony is stunning. It is bound to lift your spirits."

"Umm, yeah," I responded absentmindedly, my mind preoccupied with Anne's message.

Emily directed, signalling for me to turn right. A sense of relief mingled with apprehension as I glanced at her beautiful house."

Exhaustion weighed heavily on me, and the urgent news only added to my weariness. Without giving it much thought, I followed Emily inside, craving nothing more than some much-needed rest.

Her home resembled a queen's place and her workspace resembled a hacker's lair. Multiple laptops and tablets lay scattered about as if awaiting her command to launch a nuclear attack.

Emily offered me a seat on the sofa and found myself sinking into its soft cushions, feeling half asleep. Due to that news, I cannot even admire Emily's looks. We sat together in the morning stillness.

"So! you live alone here?"

She confided, "Actually, I live here for work. My family and relatives are in New York."

I nodded in understanding, empathizing with the challenges Emily must face living on her own. Yet, amidst our conversation, my eyes were drawn to a surprising sight – a display of gold medals adorning the wall.

Peering closely, I was surprised "You practice karate?"

Emily's response was tinged with a hint of nostalgia. "Not anymore," she admitted. "I started back in college, but I had to give it up at my mom's request."

I arched an eyebrow, intrigued by her revelation. "Your mom's request?"

Emily's reply spoke volumes about her character. "Yes," she affirmed. "She was concerned about the risk of injury. It pained her every time I got hurt."

Her dedication to her mother left a lasting impression on me. "You gave up karate because of your mom?" I echoed, struck by her sacrifice.

Emily nodded solemnly, confirming my suspicion. "When it comes to Mom, everything is worth it," she affirmed.

"Agreed." My eyes were drawn to the painting on the wall behind her, presumably of her and her father. "Is that you? How cute."

"That picture? Yes, that was me." She paused, gazing at the picture with a slightly sad expression.

"What happened, Emily?"

"You know, Robin, when I was young, my dream was to become a secret agent or a police officer. I wanted to catch thieves and bring them to justice. But I had to give up on that dream."

With each word, my admiration for her deepened. "An agent? Why?"

Emily walked over to the wall, her eyes fixed on the picture. "When I was twelve, my father was murdered during a robbery," she confessed.

My heart skipped a beat, sympathy flooding my senses. "I'm so sorry," I murmured. "It's fine," Emily replied, her tone masking the pain of her past.

"By the way, you look fit and agile, not like a typical office worker," I complimented her, trying to make her mood lighter.

"Thank you, you too, look like a gym freak." she teased, prompting me to flex my biceps before she could reach out.

We shared a laugh, our eyes meeting in a moment of shared understanding. Her gaze was captivating, her eyes sparkling with an intensity that was hard to resist. The way her eyelashes framed her eyes only added to her allure. It was a sensation unlike any other, one that made me want to draw her closer. But I quickly shifted the conversation, aware that it was too soon to be that intimate.

So, my karate kid, where is the coffee? You would not want to miss the sunrise, would you?" Emily left my bicep with a playful laugh.

"Your karate kid," she chuckled, amused by her nickname.

"Just wait a minute on the balcony, I'll be right back," Stepping onto the balcony, I was greeted by the crisp morning air and the soothing sound of chirping birds. But Anne's message still lingered in my mind. About seven minutes later, Emily returned with the coffee.

I took a sip, "Wow, Emily, this is amazing," I complimented her, genuinely impressed by her coffee-making skills. We watched the sunrise, casting a warm glow over the landscape. Emily's excitement was infectious, and I found myself caught up in the moment with her.

"Let's capture this moment," she suggested, her eyes shining with enthusiasm. "Sure, but let's make sure it doesn't hurt your boyfriend," I teased, enjoying our playful banter.

"Only if I have one," I joined in her laughter. Standing side by side, watching the sunrise, I felt a sense of peace and contentment wash over me—a feeling of connection that I had not experienced in a long time.

My phone vibrates, that's Anne "It is time to leave dear," with a smile on my face, I headed home, looking after the danger that arrived.

As I revved the engine, I called Anne, my co-undercover agent, my second and maybe final deception to Emily regarding her profession.

"Why are you dodging my calls? Are you out of your mind?" Anne's irritation seeped through the phone.

"I'm on my way, just hit a snag," I responded, my grip tightening on the steering wheel.

"No, no, forget about the office. You should spend time with her," Anne's words dripped with sarcasm, her tone leaving no room for argument.

"Are you mad, I told you last time not to track me, I will be there soon," I hastily ended the call, a sudden urgency propelling me forward.

CHAPTER THREE

Someone From the Party

Robin

"Anne you tracked me again, this was the third time." I barged into the boss's cabin.

"I would not if it was not urgent," She retorted, looking at the laptop as if nothing happened.

"Oh, enough of this," our boss George intervened. "We have more pressing matters at hand. Both of you need to focus."

"But sir..." George held up a hand and I sat beside Anne. I pinched her and she reverted with a kick under the table, like we fight always.

"I said stop it both of you, don't fight like kids." George banged the table.

"Before I show you that threatening mail, I have good news." The door opened and I saw a shadow.

"Hello everyone,"

"Deccan..." Anne almost shouted as my brother entered the room, undoubtedly stronger than before.

"Happy to see you back, brother." I embraced him. "Same brother," He hugged me back.

"Hello, Champ," Anne greeted him. "Hey, Anne."

"Welcome back, Deccan. Glad to see you after three months. Just be more careful next time," George advised.

"I would not promise sir, you know me, I hate seeing criminals roaming around freely." His injury has not changed his attitude. He settled down on a chair while flaunting his coat.

"I know, I know, I know dear. You have listed a hundred and four encounters within three years and broken laws as if it were second nature." George knew that trying to teach ethics to Deccan was a futile effort, a sheer waste of time and energy.

Meanwhile, Anne clapped for Deccan, her unwavering support evident as always. I was incredulous; killing people without a second thought was hardly a moment of pride. Whether you are at an airport, mall or anywhere, Deccan never considers the consequences.

George just smiled at him and continued "Now, I want everyone to focus on this anonymous email," we turned our attention to the TV screen.

"My dear George, how have you been? Our last encounter was rather... incomplete, thanks to Stella's timely intervention. But I warn you to be ready for the upcoming one."

"This is outrageous! Is it the killer? Is he challenging us?"My heart pounded at the sound of Stella's name, memories of that terrible day flooding back in an instant. My eyes shot to Deccan. He was still as stone, but I could see the storm brewing inside him. His eyes widened as if he had been expecting this moment as if he had been waiting for the killer to resurface. The mention of her name hit him harder than anyone else—his fists clenched, his jaw tightened, but it was the look in his eyes that shook me. There was pain there, buried deep beneath the anger, a pain that had never left him.

"Do we have any leads on where this email came from?" Deccan queried.

"Somewhere from New York, but other than this we have no clue, they've covered their tracks well," Anne responded.

"It could also be a hoax," Deccan countered looking at me for reassurance.

"But this could be a genuine threat we need to be careful." I asserted.

"Don't worry, we will approach this case just like any other. You guys can start your research and let us see how it unfolds," George ended the discussion.

"How are you feeling now?" Emily's message popped up on my phone, breaking the silence that had hung between us for a day due to this unwanted case.

"I'm doing better now, just dealing with my boss due to some burden that he gave me last minute," I replied honestly.

"I can relate, bosses are terrible," She responds in her empathetic voice.

"Don't dwell on it too much. It is Saturday. We should go out; it will help to take your mind off the things," she suggested, but a sense of disappointment rushed over my face.

"Sorry, Emily, not today. It is Anne's twenty-eighth birthday, and I have to be there as you know how she is," I explained.

"Oh, yes, your infamous friend. Birthday party, huh? Enjoy, but be prepared for her roasting session," She laughed.

"I am fully expecting it, especially since Deccan and I have to perform at the party. Roasting will be mandatory. You know I have not even rehearsed," I answered her while walking into my room.

"Deccan?" She sounds intrigued.

"Oh, I forgot to mention him. He is my elder brother," "Oh, your brother."

"Yes, he will be performing with me. Anne just sent us the videos to watch and practice the dance. Before I could refuse, Deccan accepted without a second thought."

"Wait, what? You dance too?" she asked, surprised.

"A little bit," I replied.

"Awesome! Don't forget to send me your dance video; I bet you will rock it," she encouraged me.

"Why don't you join me? You mentioned wanting to meet Anne, right?" I tried to deviate from the topic as that was too early to let her see my pathetic dance, what if she did not like it?

"No, no, no. If I come, she will make me dance and I know nothing about it," Emily declined as I knew she would.

"Don't worry, she won't,"

"I appreciate your offer Robin, but since I don't know Anne personally, so it will not look nice. Maybe next time when you introduce me at one of your parties," She suggested politely.

"Fair enough," I agreed.

"All right then, enjoy the party. Break a leg with your performance," She wished me luck before we ended the call.

I glanced at the clock and sifted through my wardrobe, sorting through an array of suits until I settled on a sleek navy blue ensemble. After mentally rehearsing the dance moves, I felt prepared for the evening ahead. With a surge of excitement coursing through me, I made my way to the sprawling farmhouse nestled deep within the seaside forest.

Anne

"Jenne, today's birthday party will have many special guests, and I want everything to be flawless. Last time, your DJ did not meet expectations, so ensure nothing goes wrong today. Double-check everything—from lighting and theme designs to the cake, party favours, and fireworks. Don't overlook any detail." I instructed my event manager.

I was amazed, after three months of absence, Deccan returned at just the right moment. Earlier, I thought he would deny coming due to what happened seventeen months back with his girlfriend Stella but not only did he show up, he agreed to perform when I asked him.

Deccan style of working is quite different from Robin's, I always wonder how can they both be brothers. Maybe because Deccan has lived away from his family from a very young age. I had always been curious about the reason, but since it is his personal life, so I never intruded.

"Oh, damn Robin, I must say eight out of ten times your clothes match your income," I laughed, he was looking dashing in his navy-blue suit with his confident grin.

"Look at yourself, walking bull, always manage to stand out in your vibrant attire." "Oh, please, at least I have some fashion sense unlike you"

"Fashion sense, huh? Even the cameraman is too busy taking pictures of other girls." Oh God, why does this man notice so much? And that cameraman—he picked the perfect moment to focus on someone else.

"Hey, can you take pictures of us? Look, people have started arriving at the doorstep, and I don't want to miss anyone." I almost shouted.

"Sure, ma'am."

"Are you ready for performance, don't cut my nose here," I looked at Robin.

"Do I need to?"

"Blah-Blah, just rehearse your moves," We bantered back and forth like always.

My eyes were searching for Deccan, and when he entered, his walk immediately caught my attention. He carried a charm in his sharp blue eyes, wearing a black coat that highlighted his muscular body and well-groomed beard. Ok, ok, stop it, Anne, I told myself, trying to control my emotions.

"Hey, Deccan, looking sharp. Ready to light up the dance floor?" I greeted him. "Ah, yes Anne." His response seemed subdued but I was happy that he came.

Meanwhile, I attended to the remaining guests including office colleagues, friends and especially our boss George. Who was busy drinking, of course, he had achieved an age where he only used to order us. I wished that I could invite my parents also, but due to office reasons and party culture, I had to celebrate with them separately.

The atmosphere was electric as we gathered for the cake-cutting ceremony, the lights casting a royal glow over the room. With each click of the camera, the vibrant energy of the celebration was captured in vivid detail. But as the time for performances arrived, all eyes were on Robin and

Deccan.

Damn, those two were on fire, their moves flawlessly executed with a confidence that commanded attention. Deccan's precision footwork and Robin's mesmerizing expressions left everyone spellbound.

"Hey, Anne, who is that guy in black?" One of my friends asked me "I like that navy one too..." Another one interrupted. They were drunk.

"Oh, shut up you guys, they are not looking for any relationships."

"Oh, Anne at least introduced us to them once." They were not backing off.

"Try to understand friends, they are gay, they cannot be with you." I felt guilty when I lied, but at least they backed off.

I did not want Robin to get a chance to taunt me on his looks, these boys should never be appreciated overly, or else they will toot their horns. Besides, I knew Deccan was not looking for any romantic entanglements at that moment.

"So, how was the performance?" Robin asked, snapping me out of my thoughts.

"You saved yourself from death," I teased, a playful grin on my lips. I took a sip of wine, and in that moment, my feelings for Deccan surged. The music, the atmosphere, his dance moves, his looks, his beard—everything seemed so lovely for a moment.

"Oh, have you even watched me properly or you were busy somewhere else?" He looked at Deccan and I immediately swatted his hand away.

"Have you finished your nonsense? There is nothing between us."

"Oh, really...?" he grinned like a Cheshire cat.

"You should see the amazing fireworks we arranged outside, against the backdrop of the sea," I suggested.

While enjoying the fireworks, I noticed Deccan was standing at a corner and quietly contemplating the night sky. Something was weighing on his mind. I excused everyone and reached out to him.

"What happened, Deccan?" I gently grabbed his arm, fighting the urge to lean in or do anything that might feel awkward. My emotions were barely in check. But I was in my senses.

"Nothing, Anne. I am fine." Sensing his uneasiness, I offered him a drink. "Thank you, Anne," He took it reluctantly and smiled.

Before I got to know the reason, George broke a glass and fell on the sofa, completely overdrunk. With Robin and Deccan springing into action to assist him, the night took an unexpected turn, leaving me frustrated by the disruption to my birthday celebration.

"He's not breathing properly, we need to get him to the hospital," Robin's urgent voice pierced through the festive atmosphere. Without hesitation, Robin and Deccan hoisted him into Deccan's car.

"What the hell, why do people overdrink if they know the risks? Spoiling both my party and mood."

CHAPTER FOUR

Brutal Past of Deccan

Robin

"How is he now?" I felt the frustration and pain in Anne's voice, her whole party got spoiled due to George's overdrinking.

"George is stable now. The doctor reassured us that he just needed some rest and we could take him back in the morning."

"Oh, so you guys have to stay there?"

"Hmm, yes Anne." She hung up abruptly, as she usually does when she is extremely frustrated.

Meanwhile, Deccan and I were in the hospital. After a long time, we finally got some moments in person.

"So, how is everything going, Deccan?"

"Fine brother, things have changed in Boston?" He responded while swapping George's test reports.

"Obviously! It has been fifteen years since you left Boston." I took away the files from him and made him focus.

"How long Deccan, how long?"

"What happened Robin?"

"You very well know what am I talking about."

"What?" He acted naive.

"About coming back home?" I came to the point.

"I told you that I don't want any discussion on this topic, don't you understand?" He snatched away the files from my hand and turned around.

"You shifted to Boston months back and still have not visited home, changed your number, like seriously brother! You know how eagerly Mom has been waiting to see you for the last fifteen years," My voice tinged with frustration.

"Don't bring up this topic again, Robin, I am warning you." He turned to me and tried to dismiss the discussion.

"Why not? You have not even provided me with your current address. Record keepers will not share your address because of your fear." I felt my voice growing louder, echoing through the sterile hospital corridor.

"You know my reasons well, Robin, now please cut the crap," he snapped his hand against the wall.

"What reasons, brother? What reasons? You did not make a single call to Dad," I retorted, my anger boiling over.

"I will never talk to him." I could see a tear forming in his eyes.

"But, brother, it has been fifteen years. Things have changed now."

"It is easy for you to say, coward, but I cannot remove those incidents from my life, never," He pushed me back.

My veins burned with anger, and I grabbed his collar tightly, pushing him towards the wall. "I am not a coward."

"You are, right from the beginning, you are. Afraid of trusting people, afraid of taking action, avoiding difficult situations. Always covering your silence with your idiotic logic."

The tension between us was palpable. Before I could say anything else, the sound of bullets echoed through the halls, and suddenly, seven or eight armed men appeared, their guns trained on us.

"We want George. Either you politely surrender, or these innocent people will die," one of them shouted. We quickly drew our weapons, aiming back at them.

"If you guys have fired one more time, trust me, I will open your cemetery right here," Deccan shouted back. God knows why this angry fellow does not use his brain. We are in a hospital; why is he instigating them?

The tension was unbearable. Nurses and patients peeked from behind corners, fear etched on their faces. The armed men did not flinch, their eyes cold and determined. The stakes were incredibly high, and one wrong move could have led to a bloodbath.

I glanced at Deccan, silently pleading for caution. We could not risk innocent lives. My mind raced, trying to find a way out of this without bloodshed.

"Listen," I said, trying to keep my voice steady. "There is no need for violence. Let us talk this out. It is a hospital."

One of the men stepped forward, his gun still raised. "You think we are here to negotiate? Just face the wall, we need George."

Deccan's grip on his gun tightened, his eyes blazing with defiance. "Deccan..." I looked at him putting my gun down.

"Are you crazy, Robin?" Despite his protest, he also put his gun down.

"You both face the wall," one of the gunmen commanded. We complied, though I kept glancing at Deccan, hoping he would not do anything rash. His eyes remained fixed on them, burning with barely contained fury.

"I said face the wall!" the gunman repeated, his gun was pointed on Deccan's head. "Deccan," I urged quietly, trying to keep the situation from escalating further.

"You two, bring George," the gunman ordered and within minutes they hurried away with George in front of us.

Deccan glared at me. "What happened, brave boy? You are not a coward, right?"

Just wait, Deccan. I'm not a fool to let them escape so easily," I whispered, a plan forming in my mind.

"What do you mean?" "Security," I called out loudly.

"Sir, we have attached the tracker on their black Mercedes, you can track it now," "What? What's going on, Robin?" His tone was laced with concern.

"Wait, Deccan. We need to follow them first," I replied, leading the way to our car as we hurriedly followed the tracker signal.

"This is my friend's hospital, I set up the security pattern here. No outsider can create chaos here," I explained as we sped through the streets.

"Then what was that? How did they get in?" his brows furrowed in confusion.

I smirked at him. "It was all part of the plan. I had a team of my best officers waiting for my signal. If I had not been here, they would have taken out the intruders without hesitation."

"Then why did you stop them?" His eyes widened in shock.

"Because we need to find out who is behind all of this. Otherwise, the game will never end,"

"Are you crazy, do you know how risky it can be, they had George, you should have killed them at that moment only."

"Drive fast, will argue later," He tightened his grip on the handle.

"We're almost there," I reassured him, gripping my gun tightly, ready for action.

"We must catch them fast. If they head into the jungle, the tracker will not work," He urged, accelerating harder.

We were just a few meters away when they opened the back gate of their car and started spilling oil on the road, causing chaos as cars began slipping and crashing into each other. Our car spun a full 360 degrees before slamming into the divider. Although we were lucky enough due to the airbags and somehow managed to get out.

"Shit, they went too far," he growled, kicking the tyre in frustration.

"Damn it," I muttered as we helplessly watched the car disappear into the jungle and with that, our chance of catching them.

We reached the office empty-handed with our shabby clothes. Having blood strains and cuts over our bodies. Our medical staff immediately brought the first aid box.

"What happened to you, why are you bleeding?" Anne was shocked, she quickly grabbed some ice water from one of the medical staff to clean Deccan's face.

"They were able to run away in front of us," I answered Anne, waiting for her to notice my presence.

"Oh, hello Robin, who ran away?"

"Some kidnappers came as mentioned in that email and they kidnapped George from the hospital. We tried to catch them, but we failed." Somewhere I felt that it was my mistake, due to which I was not able to meet Deccan's eyes.

"Relax, Robin, it is not your fault, at least you guys are safe" Anne rubbed my arm.

"It is his fault only," Deccan smashed the chair.

"What do you mean Deccan," Anne asked.

"He can stop them in the hospital itself, but no he wants to catch the man behind all this, due to which now we have nothing to chase them,"

"Robin," Anne looked at me.

"There was a plan that failed Deccan, I am sorry." I finally faced him with disappointment.

"No brother, you don't have to be sorry, I am sorry, I forgot that I was with a coward,"

"Deccan, I know you are angry but control your words."

"Why should I? You always back yourself for taking an action when required due to which we had to suffer."

"Still your tongue if you value it, Deccan. Don't act like you've never made a mistake," I snapped, the frustration boiled over my face. "Remember three months ago? You rushed into that gang fight alone, trying to play the hero, and ended up seriously injured. Anne and I were just about to catch them from the helicopter, but you charged in and botched the whole thing. We needed to interrogate them, but you encountered them and we lost our chance. That time, we lost the criminals because of your recklessness."

"So, what do you expect me to do, stay calm, and watch them run away while waiting for your helicopter? I am not like you, who cannot even stand against your father when he cheated on my mom and slapped her for the first time." Here he crossed the limits, even Anne was shocked and did not know how to react.

I grabbed his collar, "What do you mean, should I hit Dad, just like you did and run away, leaving Mom alone in that crucial time,"

"Probably after that he never tried to hit Mom," He pushed me back.

"Guys," Anne tried to stop us.

"He never hit Mom again because of her courage to stand strong and my constant support and patience."

"What support, you just want to live on dad's funds, that is why you were silent, don't say you were acting logically that time,"

"You know nothing, you think you have achieved something great after hitting Dad and leaving home. Have you ever thought about what Mom was going through when you left? You left her the moment she needed you the most, and you are also responsible for some of the million tears she got in her eyes," I sit on a chair, my neck dries out, and my eyes fill with tears.

"Till now every single drop of Mom's tears makes my heart crush apart, I was angry at Dad, but more than him I was angry at you, I am not defending him and I will never. But what you did was also not acceptable. Relationships are not like things that we can throw away if not required, they must be maintained. But for you, they are just toys to break and move forward." He did not counter me and left the room without saying anything.

"Robin, calm down," Anne held my arm, "too much happened suddenly, take some time to relax. Deccan is your brother. He is just angry a little but he loves you." I went to my cabin trying to calm myself while looking at my chess board.

I wondered how they got to know so much about us, George's name, our location, our reaction, all the loopholes, how they knew everything. These guys forced me to snatch my hair.

CHAPTER FIVE

THE MEETING

Anne

"Deccan," I shouted, rushing towards him, "Deccan stop, where are you going?" He ignored me.

"Are you listening to me?" I came in front of him, trying to stop him, but my heart skipped a beat when our eyes met.

"Are you crying, Deccan?"

"Not at all, Anne, just leave me for a moment."

"No, I will not." I wrapped around his arms. He was in pain.

"Anne, I am fine." He gently moved my arms aside, looking into my eyes.

"You should be with Robin. He is upset; talk to him, he needs you. I was too harsh on him." His eyes reflected the regret he felt over what had happened with Robin.

"He is fine, he is not a kid anymore. Moreover, he uses his mind. I am worried about you, who took action then think and regret."

"He was not a coward Anne, he is grown that way, mom always taught us to avoid fights, she told us that we have to know the consequences."

"Then why are you like this?" He paused and took me towards the office balcony.

"Anne, I still cried for that moment when I smashed Dad with a bat. No matter how he was, he is my father." He coughed.

"You need water?"

"No." He held the railing and continued, "That day was horrible, when mom got to know about Robin's father's affair, she talked with him, but he did not listen to her, he showed the power of his money, and wanted to make her quiet. He treated us like a slave with his words and shouted to the extent that even Robin cried, he was a child. But my patience level broke when he grabbed my mom's neck and smashed her to the wall, I saw a tear from her eyes when her eyes met mine."

"You know what Anne, my mom gave everything to our family, she sacrificed her dreams, her likes, even her life for us. She worked like a slave throughout those seventeen years when I saw her. Treated Robin's father like a god. But that moment, when I saw tears from her eyes, my heart broke into thousands of pieces, I wished to die before seeing her like this again. I took my bat and smashed it. Trust me Anne that day if there was any other person in the place of him, I would have killed him without any second thought." His eyes turned red.

"I know it's not my place to speak, but he is your father too, Deccan. Don't be too hard on him."

"I am sorry, but I can't."

"And then you left alone?"

"I told my mom to come with me, there is no point in stating where you felt disrespected, but she refused, she refused because of Robin." I was not able to react. I never saw Deccan like this.

"But how did you manage to live alone, you left without any planning?"

"I was not completely on my own. I had a friend in New York, my old schoolmate and gaming partner, who had moved there for his father's business expansion. I stayed with him and his family. They were incredibly supportive, helping me with my studies and everything else. But New York was dangerous back then, with crime rates soaring. My delivery salary was snatched twice, pushing me to learn how to fight and defend myself."

"Deccan..." I hugged him, I had no words to say at that moment.

Robin

I was scrolling my head while looking at my chessboard and felt quite guilty after that serious conversation with Deccan, I never wanted to make this conversation in that way. It had been only seventeen months since he had lost Stella, the love of his life and our fellow agent. The way she handled the IT department, no one had ever done. If she were alive today then by this time, we would know about the place where the mail came from along with the kidnappers' location and everything. She was a brilliant girl, she knew how to control Deccan, maybe her death was also a reason behind the rise in such aggressive behaviour of Deccan.

Anne and Deccan entered my cabin.

"Robin, you need some apple juice?" Anne offered me juice.

"You are offering me apple juice, that too with a smile. Are you ok?" I laughed, but my eyes still ignored Deccan, I did not know how to face him.

"You don't want it, ok fine."

"Oh, no, no give it to me. Finally, something will go inside after twelve hours." I took a sip without any second thought.

"It is warm Anne,"

"Wait, let me mix some ice," Before she went towards the fridge. "Anne," I stood up from my chair, "Juice"

"Yes, coming,"

"No, the drinks at your party, maybe George did not drink much, maybe someone mixed something in his drink?"

"Possible," We shared glances.

"We have to check every single camera of your farmhouse, also the list of candidates who have attended your party, even workers."

"It will take some time, let me check," She started scrolling up her laptop. "I got a message, we have got their black car," Deccan looked at Anne

"Great, did you find something?" Anne asked and I finally looked at Deccan.

"No, only George's fingerprints were there in the car, they might have changed their vehicle in the mid-jungle,"

"Oh," Anne was disappointed.

"Now the only clue is the party footage." I interrupted and Anne started her search again.

"Do you need any help?" Deccan asked, approaching the laptop. Still simmering with anger and guilt, I could not bear to be around him and I turned and walked out of the room, needing some fresh air to cool off.

After a long, exhausting night at the hospital and a fight with Deccan, I finally had a moment for myself. I glanced at the clock; it was 1 PM. I pulled out my phone and messaged

Emily, "What are you doing?"

After around five minutes, I received her message, "Actually I have a half day today, so just heading for home in a few minutes."

"Oh! that's great, let's meet somewhere, what say?"

"You are free today, what about your work?" She asked.

"I have completed my today's work. So, I am free now"

"Oh, we can meet but where?"

"It is a surprise. Tell me where you are, and I will pick you up."

"Surprise, for me? Why?" She laughed.

"Why not, you are my buddy right,"

"Yeah, yeah, buddy, but tell me please where are we going?" Her excitement was genuine but I had not planned anything, that word "surprise" was spontaneous.

"Hmm, ok you make a guess."

"Are we going to that new Citadel mall in town? It is supposed to be beautiful. My friends told me about the sales of top brands and the food courts there." She was very excited about it and expectedly, I got the place where she wanted to go.

"Oh great, you guessed it right in the first go, amazing."

"Seriously? We are going there? Wonderful."

"Great, send me your location, I will be there soon." I messaged her with a smiley emoji at the end.

"Oh, no worries, I am near the mall, we can meet directly at the mall."

"Sure." I ended the call and quickly sifted through my office wardrobe, throwing on a black jacket over my white t-shirt and baggy jeans.

"What are you taking for her?" Anne popped up suddenly. "Hey, don't you know you do not listen to other private talks?"

"Private talks..., nice Robin. But you are an asshole, you did not even tell me that you are going on a date?"

"It is not a date, Anne." I tied up my shoes and put on some Versace Eros.

"Kind of start, what's her name?" She picked up my Rado watch.

"Give it back, Anne, I'm getting late."

"Nope, tell me first."

"Emily." I snatched my watch back.

"Emily, nice. So, what are you taking for her?"

"It is not our date. What if she takes it wrong or does not like it."

"Why would she? As a friend, you can take something."

"I don't know about her preferences yet."

"You think she will tell you to bring her something? Girls like it when guys put in effort, especially when it is not asked for. I am not saying you to act like a boyfriend, just be genuine. Take something thoughtful. Or don't, it is your choice, hell is always open for guys like you." Sometimes I failed to understand Anne's mood swings. She left with a sudden statement and created a dilemma for me, whether to take a gift for Emily or not. So, I decided to check something in the mall only.

CHAPTER SIX

THE MALL UNDER FIRE

Robin

I reached the mall and called her, "Where are you, I am entering from the main gate,"

"Look at your right. " She looked fabulous in a white top, jacket, and pants as she approached me.

"Hi Emmi" I greeted her with a handshake.

"Emmi," she chuckled. What a coincidence—a black jacket over white, looking great." She praised me.

"Thank you, same to you."

"Thanks, wait a second," Her eyes moved towards my arm then to my face, "What happened? Did you have an accident or something?" She touched my arm gently.

"Oh, it is nothing. My brother is a rash driver, so our car did a three-sixty-degree spin in a small accident."

"Three-sixty degrees! When did this happen?"

"Last night, on our way back from Anne's birthday party."

"You guys should avoid drinking while driving, It's not safe."

"Oh, no Emily, we did not drink at all. It was just my brother's adrenaline rush, driving over 150 km/hr."

"Adrenaline rush seriously, 150 km/hr, Is he okay?"

"Yes, yes, we are both fine. Do not worry. Tell me where you want to go first?" I tried to calm her.

"Robin," Her eyes were filled with concern.

"Yes, Emily?"

"Be careful next time. It is not a joke that you are smiling about."

"Sure, Emily. I will be more careful. Don't spoil your mood now." I held her shoulders.

"Fine, let's visit the games room first." Finally, the topic shifted, and we moved on.

"You like games?"

"I love games, although, after my stupid job and stupid colleagues, I could not get in the mood to play."

"Stupid colleagues," I looked at her to know more. "Yes, I won't get much time because of them."

"No worries, you can play freely today"

"Yeah," We entered the game zone and somehow her mood got lighter.

Her excitement was like a free kid who wants to enjoy, who wants to fly in this world. Damn, she was looking very cute, we played cricket, rode a car together, copy the funny expressions presented in the mirror, and the way she laughed, was the awesome part of that evening.

"Let us play shooting Robin, you like shooting?"

"Yes, I love it."

"Shit just missed the center." She was a good shooter I must say, almost at the center, but then it was my turn, I had to miss some shots to maintain my fake identity and I did so.

"Not bad Robin, you will learn it slowly after some practice."

"Yes, yes truly why not you teach me a little?"

"Oh, it is very easy to see let me adjust the angle for you" She covered me from the back, her hands were above mine handling the gun, and my hands shivered a little as I felt her breath.

"Now shot."

"Wow, almost at the center Emily, you see." She was smiling but a little glimpse of disappointment covered her face.

"What happened Emily, you are not happy?"

"I am Robin, but I always wished to win that teddy once, I tried many times, but I always ended close." My heart melted looking at her innocent face.

"Emily, why don't you try one more time?" I offered her the gun.

"No, Robin, it is over now, it was way more difficult than I thought." That time I felt like shooting at every single target at that shop and winning all those teddy bears for her.

"Just one more time please, take it." I went aside as she aimed at the target, the moment before she was about to shoot, I moved her hand with a slight force.

"Are you ok, Robin?"

"Yes, yes, just lost my balance, these carpets suck."

"Congratulations, ma'am, you hit the target, what teddy do you want?" The store owner looked at her.

"What, I won. Robin look, I won." That smile on her face was worthy.

"Oh! You did it Emily, I told you that you can." She was so excited that she hugged me and my mind stuck at that moment.

As we moved forward, my eyes were on her smile, when she stopped suddenly.

"Robin, look..." Emily pointed to a little girl standing silently, looking somewhere.

"Hey girl, why are you so silent what happened?" I asked.

"I want that toy that uncle has." The girl said softly.

"Toy? What toy? There's no toy," I replied, confused.

"I just saw that white shirt uncle hide a toy gun in her back." We looked at that person. He was talking over the phone.

"Are you sure you saw a toy gun," I asked to confirm.

"Yes, uncle, I am sure." The moment turned tense.

Without hesitation, Emily knelt down, handing the girl her teddy bear. "Here, take this. Forget about that toy. Where are your parents?"

The girl pointed across the corner. "There is my mom."

"Go on, run to her, and enjoy the bear." I admired Emily's quick thinking as the girl smiled, thanked her, and hurried off. The moment she left, I instinctively checked for my gun.

"Robin, listen stay quiet, if that guy has a gun, then probably he is not alone, he enters here passing the security, which means someone from the security is involved with him, which can be a problem." Emily's innocence turned into a mature agent.

"He can be anyone, maybe a bodyguard, a police officer, or a criminal." She suggested.

"His clothes do not justify the professions. Still, we cannot leave him alone."

"Robin, look there."

"What?" I followed her gaze.

"That man just gives some signals to that ice cream seller" "There may be more people then" I looked at Emily.

"What can be their motive today, a connection with the security guard, are they planning to loot the mall, no very difficult, you cannot escape from here so easily, there is a police station nearby, moreover they are in twenty-four-seven camera footage. The matter is different."

"Are they planning to kidnap someone?" she suggested.

"But why do they choose a weekday, if they want to kidnap any random kid then weekends will be the best, and if they want to kidnap any specific person then why from the mall, it can be better done outside the mall, where you can kidnap and run easily."

"Robin, what if they want to kill someone?"

"Can be true, but again the same thing, it can be better done outside the mall?"

"What if he is an important person having too much security and can only be killed when a party with his family members surrounds him?" I was impressed by her sudden logical answers.

"But, do we have any party here today?"

"Yes, we have, when we entered, I read on the board that the Anniversary party of Mr. William is on the second floor. Maybe he is the one."

"Mr William that famous builder?"

"Can be, he can easily afford this and can be a good target for anyone whether his competitors or any other."

Wow, wow, wow, the way Emily used her brain in the last couple of minutes, makes me admire her more. I was like, is she the same girl I have been dealing with for the past half an hour, playing games and enjoying like a kid?

"Wow, Emily, you are a perfect fit to be an agent."

"No time for compliment, we should hurry up and check."

"Let me go to the party and you should go to the security room do let me know if you find something odd."

"Sure" Without wasting time we rushed, I entered the party, and she headed towards the security room, we were connected on call.

"They have hacked the cameras."

"What the hell."

"Let me just try to check it, you better stay careful, I am also sending these two guards there. How many bodyguards does the builder have there?"

"Let me check, around three, we cannot involve ground security because anyone from them can be involved in this."

"True."

I looked around we were almost six people to save William. I meet him. "Sir, your life can be in danger, just be careful."

"Who are you?"

I had to show him my card to trust me. "Oh, my friend also works in special cops."

"Oh, which one..." bang suddenly two bullets fired on the ceiling. I took out my gun and all the guards covered William.

In the span of half a minute, two waiters took out guns pointing at us, two people came from the main gate and three were just below the stage having a clear shot at us. Damn it.

Firing started, I was very careful while shooting so that no innocent got harmed.

I knocked out one, meanwhile, one of our guards also knocked out one. But they were very sharp and able to knock three of our guards. We somehow managed to take William down the stage, then suddenly our one more man got down. I killed two of them, and then it is three vs two of us. Meanwhile, I was aiming for one more when suddenly a gunshot at my hand, my gun dropped, it was hard enough to make a severe cut. As the blood dropped on the floor, I quickly looked at them, but the bullet did not come from those three, it was from the one behind me the bodyguard and he went towards William, I stood to stop him, but one of the three gunmen came to me a drag me to the wall, he banged my head hard to the decorative painting, I received around three punches in a go, but I manage to dodge the fourth one and punched back on the stomach, I grabbed his head and threw him on glass table.

But it was late everything happened so instantly. The crowd was left and Willam was killed by them. They all escaped pointing the guns towards me. I somehow handled myself and reached toward William, meanwhile, Emily ran toward me.

"Robin, are you ok?" She was breathing heavily.

"I am fine, let's go to the office, this is not a simple case." She looked tense, we reached the car.

"Let me drive, Robin" I nodded.

"I cracked the security camera but they were way advanced, I somehow managed to get a few footage."

"We will check them at the office." I took out some tissues and tried to hold the blood.

"But what can we do with those footage?"

"We will try to look for that bodyguard, I remember a slight of his face, maybe I had seen him somewhere, and the video may reveal him. We have to see the vehicle from which they ran away, I have taken pictures of all the security guards. We will interview them later."

"I never knew that you have a gun?" In the hurry of this case, I almost forgot about my lie to Emily, but the way she asks looks like she knew something but pretended to avoid it.

"Gun, that is for protection purposes." I wiped my sweat.

"But the way you fought shows like you are a professional shooter." She laughed a little.

"Robin," she held my arm and came closer looking towards me, sharing a glance at me.

"Yes, Emily," I heard how awkward I sounded.

"If you are hiding something from me then it is the best time to tell me, I trust you and I am there for you till the time you trust me." The way she said made me feel guilty and I felt for her more.

"Emily, actually,"

"Ok, no worries, take your time." We reached the office, I stopped the car and looked at her.

"I am sorry, I lied to you about my profession, I am not a marketing consultant." With a heavy breath I continue, "I am an..."

"An agent." She held my hand.

"How do you...?" I went a little back.

"When I first time saw your profile and searched about you, I found your professional details a little fishy, and suddenly I checked that some people started scrolling for my details. I get to know that you are not a common man." She blew my mind away.

"What, you know it well enough," My eyes winded up "Somewhere I doubt it, but I get it completely today."

"Then why did you come today, why are you still here when you knew that I lie?"

"Because I never saw a stranger to care this much, boarding a flight to clear a misunderstanding, helping that driver with money, helping me in winning that teddy without even showing, being so genuine." She held my arms, "Robin, you make me feel like I matter to you. Therefore, I listened to my heart this time and trusted you, to wait for you to tell me the truth."

"I want to tell you about my profession Emily but..."

"I know you cannot because you have to follow the rules." She came a little closer "I trust you and I am there with you Robin." She winked.

"Emily..." I settle her hair behind her ears. Several emotions rushed through me and I wanted to hug her hard, but all I said was, "Thank you, Emily." And went out of the car.

CHAPTER SEVEN

Is She the Right Choice?

Robin

We entered the office, "Hey, Anne" I avoided Deccan.

"Hey Robin..." they both looked at Emily with a suspicious look.

"Why are you bleeding, what happened?" Deccan came closer to check me, but I stepped back.

"Robin got injured in a fight," Emily responded on my behalf.

"You are Emily, right?" Anne confirmed.

"Yes, Anne."

"And you are here because?"

"Anne, I will answer your questions but first call some medical staff, Robin is bleeding," Emily answered in a rush.

"Go, Anne, call someone." Deccan teased Anne. It was one of those rare moments when a stranger ordered Anne. She shot a horrified look at me.

"Emily helped me, Anne." I interrupted before Anne made any comment.

She called the staff over the phone and looked at me "Robin can I talk with you for a moment." I knew what it was for, so I excused Emily and went into the cabin.

"Are you fucking crazy, who the hell is she to order me, moreover, what is she doing here, don't you know we cannot bring our relations into the office and we cannot even tell them about our profession?" She held my hand so tight that it pains more than the bullet.

"Anne, Anne calm down, I know everything, let me tell you something, Emily is here to help us."

"Help us, how?" she tightened her grip.

"She is an excellent ethical hacker, I saw her presence of mind when we were in the mall, she helped me almost to solve a case."

"Case?"

"Yes, Mr. William that famous builder got killed by some gunmen in the mall, we tried our best but our efforts went in vain." She finally released my hand.

"How many were there?"

"Around seven and I think someone from the security is also with them else it was not possible to enter a mall with so many guns."

"Have you checked the security cameras?" She applied medicine to my wound.

"Ouch," I winced. "Yes, we did, but those people were not common gunmen. They were professionals, and their hacking skills were amazing."

"Same as the person who came to my party."

"What do you mean?"

"The video clip of my party has not shown up, some error is coming repeatedly." She opened her laptop and showed me that error.

"Maybe Emily can help."

"Robin please, it is not a cybercrime, it is a criminal case, our professional hackers also failed to crack it and you think she can do it?"

"What if she can, will you let her join us?"

"What? Are you serious? Don't be mad in love."

"No, not at all, see Anne," I said, guiding her to a chair. "You know how badly we were searching for an ethical hacker after the death of Stella. Still, we were unable to find a suitable one. You know we recruit people based on our research into various companies, backgrounds, and individual motives. We cannot just advertise for job roles. Emily is one of the best hackers that we need, I believe in her. Give her a chance."

"What about her background?"

"You can do whatever formalities it will take. Interview her, get your answers, and hire her if you feel confident, ok?" She paused for a moment.

"Hmm, ok it will work," Anne called both and showed the computer screen to Emily.

"Emily, can you crack this error, we have to see the footage in it."

"I can try, Robin, but are you ok now?"

"Yes, I am fine now, don't worry, give me that footage you have taken from the mall," I assured her, and she started her work.

"What footage?" Deccan looked at Anne.

"Someone was killed at the mall today, it is regarding the same," Anne answered back, while I played that clip.

"He will be here only, look there is he, the killer." I zoomed at his face.

"He dared to kill, without even hiding his face?" Deccan was shocked. We looked further.

"Oh, shit, Deccan look at this." I finally talked with him.

"Yes Robin, it is the same black Range Rover with a different number that we found in the forest," He confirmed.

"Oh, I remember Mr. William told me that he knew someone from our office, but before he could complete firing started."

"Deccan you know something about him?" Anne looked at Deccan.

"No, I don't know him."

"Even I don't know?" They looked at me.

"Maybe George?" I suggested.

"Possible, let's take another look at that bodyguard. Maybe we will find something more," Anne suggested, replaying the clip.

"What seriously?" We were shocked.

"The cameraman," we confirmed together.

"Cameraman?" Deccan was confused.

"Yes, he was the cameraman at my party, I remember his face when I scolded him."

"Anne, from where did you hire him, contact him now." All the dots are connecting somewhere.

"Let me contact my event manager, Jenne," she went out to call her to find out about the cameramen. Our clear suspect and hope to get to the kidnappers.

"I am sorry," Deccan whispered.

"What, what did you say?" I asked, thinking my ears had deceived me. Deccan apologized.

"I am sorry Robin, no matter how angry I was I should not scold you like that, you are my little brother, you have achieved a lot, solved many cases, and that is why you are here today. I should not argue with you like that." His words are touching, although he is a hot-headed idiot but still, he is my brother. Who gains emotions once a year.

"I am sorry too for being rude, forget about it now." I ended on a lighter note and hugged him.

Anne arrived, "Jenne sent us the details of that cameraman, she said that he provided her with the videos and photos of the event. She will share that shortly."

"Great, we have to reach out to him." Deccan assisted.

Meanwhile, Emily came with the laptop. "The footage is cracked we can see it now," I quickly reached to see Anne's reaction.

"You have cracked it?" Anne was shocked.

"Yes." She handed over the laptop to Anne and we turned on the footage.

"Damn, that cameramen mixed something in the drink and served it to George." Anne banged the table.

"Can we turn up the volume?" I looked at Emily.

"Here it is." She clicked some keys and played the footage again.

"Sir, here is your special wine, let's have a picture of you holding a wine, it is a fashion nowadays."

"Oh, thank you so much."

"This aged George, is he a fool or something, he is our senior still he falls into this trap."

"Calm down Anne, we could not do anything, it was a secret agent's party, and everyone was enjoying it, in such cases, it is difficult to catch such small things." Deccan calmed her down.

"We have to catch this cameraman as soon as possible," He replied.

"Great work Emily," We shared a smile. I love that Emily cracked out the video, she is a well-deserving agent.

"Yes, great work Emily," Anne and Deccan also appreciated her.

"Emily, can I talk to you for a second?" I asked. Anne and Deccan exchanged glances and left the room, giving us some privacy. The moment the door closed behind them; I couldn't hold my happiness. I held her shoulders, grinning widely. "You did it, Emily. You did it!"

"Thank you, Robin,"

"Ok, now I want to ask you one thing."

"Yes, Robin?" She looked a little nervous.

"You always want to be an agent, right?"

"Amm, yes."

"So, do you want to join us, Agent Emily?" I looked into her eyes.

"An agent..." She got excited but her excitement went down suddenly, she looked down "But Robin I am a hacker only. How can I?"

"You are not an ordinary hacker Emily, you are great, we all saw your work, it is amazing, you crack the video that none of our professionals could."

"But Robin, what about mom?"

"Look into my eyes, Emily." I gently lifted her chin with my fingers, "This is your call. Think it over carefully. It is true that if you decide to join us, you cannot tell anyone—not your mom, not even your sister. This is your dream, and You are more than capable of achieving it. That's why I'm asking you to consider it. Don't worry about your current job; we'll create a demo ID for you in our demo company to cover everything."

"Robin..." She hugged me hard tears filled her eyes.

"Robin, I will remember this throughout my life, you have, you have..." She hugged me again.

"Oh, Emily." She got overwhelmed.

"Now, Anne will talk with you, she has to do some formalities, just face her a little." We laughed.

CHAPTER EIGHT

THE NEXT VICTIM

Robin

We four went to Jenne's office the next morning in search of that cameramen. We entered the room and without any greetings, Anne said, "Jenne, where is the cameraman,"

"What happened Anne, is everything alright, you need water or something?" She stood up.

"Jenne, we need to meet the cameraman who shot my birthday party."

"You mean Steve, what happened, did he do something wrong?"

"Ma'am, can you please tell us where he is?" Deccan interrupted.

"Hmm, sure," She called the reception, "Send Steve into my cabin."

"He is coming." We were looking at the door to meet that jerk. A man of around thirty-one entered the room.

"There he is." Jenne identified him as the cameraman.

"You are..." I looked at him closely.

"He is not the man we are looking for." I checked for Anne's reaction.

"Last Saturday, did you come to my villa for the shot?" Anne moved towards him.

"Hmm, yes." His hands were shaking.

"He is lying" Deccan held his collar and stuck him on the wall, "Either you speak the truth or I will make every single bone of your body dance like hell."

"Deccan leave him,"

"Stay away Robin."

"Tell the truth or he will surely kill you," Anne warned him and he nodded.

"Deccan, leave him." I held his hand and he left him on the floor.

"Sorry sir, I am sorry, I got greedy when he offered me five thousand dollars,"

"Who gave you five thousand dollars?"

He cleared his throat, "Sir, he met me last Saturday just before the entrance of the party and asked me for my ID, without a second thought he gave me five thousand dollars and told me not to tell anyone about it. I was scared earlier but I saw a gun with him and if I refused his offer then he might shoot me at that moment, so I accepted and went home."

"You..."

"Deccan stop now, hitting him is useless" I urged and showed him the picture of that fake cameraman.

"Yes, yes, he is the one."

"There was no point in wasting more time here." We went towards our car.

"What the hell, we went back to zero the only clue we have was the cameramen who was also fake." I was disappointed, but Emily held my arm, "Everything will be fine Robin, relax."

"Even media has also telecasted the murder case of Willam,"

"Don't worry Robin, they have nothing to show instead of after-crime pictures." Emily consoled me.

"Anne, circulate the picture of that killer among our trusted agents, we have to catch him soon."

"Yes, Robin. I will share it as soon as we get to the office."

I glanced at Deccan, gripping the handle tightly and driving in silence. "You okay, Deccan?" I asked, but he just nodded, focused on the road. When we finally arrived at the office, everyone was waiting for us.

"What happened guys?"

"There is a parcel for you Robin." I opened it as we reached my cabin. That was from our main headquarters, the senior team of all other agent groups that ran across the states

"There is a clip. Anne, can you play it."

"Sure."

"Hello, Robin. It is disheartening to hear about the kidnapping of George. He is one of our sharpest and most dedicated agents. Robin, you must find him at any cost. This is a matter of our collective security. You are the lead now, assemble your team and take this case further."

"Congratulations, Robin." Everyone clapped with a little admiration.

"Congratulations Brother, sorry, team lead!" Deccan hugged me tight.

Being appointed as a team lead is an incredible opportunity, a testament to the organization's trust in me. However, it also means the pressure has doubled. The weight of finding George now rests squarely on my shoulders.

"Guys, it is time to work harder. Anne, you can circulate the picture now."

"Sure, just a minute." Anne reached for her laptop, but before she could open it, a subordinate knocked on the door.

"Yes?"

"Sir, a delivery boy came with this parcel for you."

"Another parcel, but I have not ordered anything, have you scanned it properly?"

"Yes sir."

We looked at each other, "Ok bring it up" Anne took that black box and put that on the table. When she opened it, she got scared and fell back.

"Be careful." Deccan held her and looked towards the box that smelled like hell. "What is this, a finger?" Emily exclaimed, recoiling, and covering her nose.

"It is George's finger; I remember this diamond ring that he flaunts every time."

"A pen drive is also there." Deccan picked up that pen drive and gave it to Anne.

"There is a video inside."

"Play it."

"That's him, the killer."

"Robin, look there," I followed Deccan's hand, "There is George forcefully sitting on an ice cube."

"Hello my dear Robin, hope you are fine now. You are searching for me, right? Ok let me give you a chance, if you can catch me then I promise I will surrender. My next target will be Peter Austin, the famous movie director, who will come to Boston the day after tomorrow as a chief guest for an emerging Model fashion show. He will die soon after the models complete their walk. Remember, it will be between us, don't try to cancel the event or involve your other agents,

or else you know that George still has nine fingers left. Your one mistake will cost him two fingers, be careful."

"How can he know us? He knew everything, our place, our actions, our names. We must be careful it can be a trap to follow what he says." Anne suggested.

"I think we should share his details with our agent's network, we have to kill him." Deccan looked at me.

"No, Deccan we cannot, he has George and we cannot take his life at risk."

"Robin, trust me, do you really think this person will leave George, no, he will kill him as soon his mission gets accomplished, he is just wasting our time."

"Deccan, we have no idea what his mission is or why he is killing these people. We do not have any other option. If we don't follow his instructions, we'll lose our lead. We must take this chance."

"But Robin, he knew that we would come there, so it can be dangerous for us." Anne's eyes filled with tension.

"Hmm, yes, guys it will be risky, we cannot go there together. The way he claimed that Peter would be killed just after the walk means it might be possible that someone from the model would be involved in this."

"So, what is your plan, Robin?" Deccan asked, meanwhile, my eyes met Emily, I quickly closed the box and sprayed the room freshener all over.

"Are you ok, Emily?"

"Better now."

"Take a sip of water." I suggested meanwhile, Anne being Anne, "You have to get habitual of all this smell, Emily."

"Anne, let her take her time." Deccan gently held Anne's back.

"Ok, so the plan is we go separately, Anne and Emily, you will participate in that walk. To look after others."

"Will love to do it. After months got some opportunity to feel better."

"Control Anne, don't forget your mission there."

"I know Robin relax it will be a cakewalk for me."

"But not for me, guys," Emily interrupted, her scared face making me laugh a little. "I never did acting and all. How can I perform in a fashion show? There will be a lot of cameras, and lots of people. I will surely mess it up."

Before I say something. Anne assured in her way, "Oh relax Emily, I will be there for you, I will sort all the things. Why not participate when you have a model face."

"But Anne..."

"Oh no if but, we are going there and it is final."

"But how can we participate, we have not filled out the form?"

"That will be easy, we have connections there, it will not be an issue." Emily looking at me, she will surely kill me for this.

"Ok then, Deccan and I will look after the stage area."

"Sure." Deccan left the room.

"Let me go and prepare for the event, I think you both should also take some rest." Anne left with a teasing look. God knows when she will use her brain.

"You, you, you idiot..." Emily hit me hard.

"What happened," I defended while laughing.

"You know I cannot perform still you created this trouble for me, do you even know the level of the crowd the function will have? What will I do, how will I walk with all eyes on me?"

"Relax Emily, Anne will be there for you."

"Anne seriously..." She held her head.

"Oh, don't stress, Emily," I tried to reassure her, but my laughter betrayed me.

"You laugh one more time and I will kick you."

"Dear Emily, what is the problem?"

"What's the problem? Do you want to know more? Tell me what will I wear for that walk? What if my makeup goes wrong? What if I slip while walking?"

"Emily," I held her shoulders gently, "Take a deep breath first. Now look into my eyes and tell me, what do you see?"

"Death!" Her expression was enough to make me fall for her.

"Emily, I trust you. You can do this and I want you to step out and see the potential within you and let it shine," I urged, drawing upon all my motivational skills that day.

Emily

How easily he said that I could do it. God knows what will happen, I want to become an agent, an agent who works behind the notice of people. But Robin, despite knowing the fact that how poor I am in this modelling and limelight things, allotted me a task to perform on one of the biggest model fashion shows, not only this, I had to deal with Anne, who will no doubt try to bring a model out of me and during this process, I don't know how many times I will get scolded.

My heart was racing as our car moved towards the death location. "Excited, Emily?" Anne put her hand over my neck, which felt so heavy that I could slip anytime.

"Anne, my dear, I am nervous, can't I do something else? Maybe I could be the stylist for the models?" I looked at her, hoping she would understand my anxiety and offer some reassurance.

"Oh, please no more crying face Emily, see how beautiful you look, you have seen the videos I gave you yesterday?"

"Yes, but..." Videos, she thought videos were enough to learn something in one day.

"Then no need to worry, just do it like that, it will be a five-minute thing."

"Ahh, okay..." I sighed, realizing there was no point in arguing with Anne. She had made up her mind to make me walk that day whether I liked it or not. It was just a five-minute thing, but for those five minutes, I had to prepare my mind for five hours. Finally, I surrendered, accepting that I had no other choice.

The car stopped so did my thoughts "We cannot enter together, you guys should go first, where the model's room, we will be there shortly." Robin looked at us and went inside.

As we reached the hall, I saw more than two lakh people, including fashion influencers, wholesalers, retailers, designers, vloggers, etc, were there to capture that moment. Even the sunshine cannot beat the level of lightning the hall has. Around forty cameramen are ready to shoot each angle of the walk today. After looking and asking here and there we finally reached the dressing room, where I saw a lot of beautiful faces, seriously they looked like professional fashion show models.

"Anne, what do we have to wear?" I asked, gazing at the array of designer clothes in front of me.

"Just wait, the coordinator will tell us."

"Ms Anne..." The coordinator called out her name.

"Yes, here I am," Anne responded eagerly, almost sprinting toward the coordinator as she had just won the runway.

"Here are your clothes, you will go number twenty-four. Be ready."

"Hmm, ok, do you have more dresses to offer?" Anne asked as she got a black mini dress, just above her knees. She wanted to check out more.

"No, since you are the last-moment entries, we left with these two that fit you." Anne being Anne, anyway accepted it.

"And you are..." She looked at me.

"She is Emily," Anne replied.

"Here is yours, you will go number ten."

"Number ten!" she gave me a red velvet dress, falling below the surface and having both side slits and left.

"Anne, can you please help me to get ready, I have to go number ten." I forgot to observe others, my mind was filled with the walk only.

"Yeah, yeah, go and change, I will wait outside, if you need any help, do tell me."

I entered the changing room, handling the dress carefully, the fabric was so smooth that it slipped every time I tried to tie the knots.

"Anne..." I called out her name, "Anne," but she was not responding, in a hurry, I opened the door and pulled her inside holding her hand.

"I told you to be..." Shit, shit, shit, shit.

"Oh, wonderful dress Emily."

"Robin, what are you doing here? Where is Anne?"

"I came to see you both and she left me here, said that in case you need any help?"

This girl, "I don't need your help, just go and call Anne immediately."

"No, I will not."

"What, Robin this is not the fun time, I have to go number ten and I have to dress up fast and do some make-up, adjust my hair, tie these knots, plus if anyone sees you here with me will be a new trouble..."

"Shh..." He put a hand on my mouth and very smoothly tied up the knots of the dress, with his eyes stuck with mine.

"You look more beautiful when you get tensed." I was unable to react. He gently took me towards the wall, his smell, and his eyes somewhere created magic in me. His hands slide on my arm. But before it goes further.

"Emily..." The bull shouted and we were back off.

"Oh, sorry did I disturb you both, no worry you guys carry on. We will catch the murderer next time."

"Anne, I was helping her." He left my hand.

"I know your help very well," She taunted and looked at me, "Looking so cute Emily." She was ready with her dress.

"Are you sure?"

"Yes, that's true, all the best." Robin complimented and left the room.

I adjusted my hair and turned towards Anne, "Anne, where had you gone, without even telling me?"

"Emily, I doubt a lady there in the golden black dress, she is the one who switched her position with you to go last on the ramp walk. She is not focusing much on her make-up or dress or walk, she is just roaming here and there and observing things."

"Oh, it might be possible that she will have some trouble on stage, you should go and inform Robin about this."

"Yes, till the time, keep following her." I nodded.

CHAPTER NINE

ALMOST CAUGHT HIM

Robin

"Deccan, Anne told me about a suspect model in the changing room, but we still have to be careful, because it will be difficult for a model to do something on stage in front of so many cameras, the real danger might be someone from outside, having a connection with her."

"We have to work on possibilities, are you ready Robin?"

"Yes, I am covering the stage area, and you?"

"I am near Peter's chair, If I find something, I will let you know," He assured me.

"Sure."

"Ladies and gentlemen put your hands together for our guest of honour, Mr Peter Austin."

The crowd applauded as he entered the hall through the main gate with a walking stick in his left hand, a hearing aid under his long brown hair, and typical old-fashioned glasses that justified his age in his late forties. I looked at Deccan, who followed him. We could not tell Peter that his life was at risk, or else we would lose George. But we were determined not to let him die. Deccan was there with him meanwhile I was looking at every moment of interaction Peter made with people.

He settled down in his chair, everything seemed fine. The judges had arrived, and the entries had also started. I was alert and worried about his life, but on the other hand, I was happy that Emily would perform today, which was quite the opposite of her nature.

There she was, entering nervously, but the way she walked, she commanded attention, taking my eyes completely on her. That red velvet dress flaunted over her legs and her collarbones adding beauty to her. But the moment was interrupted by a sudden bark of a dog. I had no idea where the dog had come from, but it caused a commotion in the hall. I turned around and heard another voice, this time from Peter, who got infuriated with a staff member for splitting coffee over him.

"Sorry sir sorry, that dog bark scared me off." The staff member insisted on cleaning him up meanwhile Deccan took Peter to the washroom. The ramp walk continues and Peter joins after a couple of minutes. Looked fit and fine.

Anne arrived after a few entries, flaunting as if she came here for the walk only, the way she posed, ignoring us, and facing the camera. I don't know what happened to this girl, whenever she gets a chance to act, she forgets everything.

Then came the final walk of the evening. I scanned the surroundings for any signs of trouble as mentioned by the killer, but everything seemed normal until the walk ended. As soon as the walk ended Peter fell, Deccan and I rushed to see him, and the moment we held him up we saw blood running through his ears and nose.

Deccan checked him, "he is dead."

"How can this be possible I saw myself no one was here, no one touched him, and even you are with him throughout the event."

"Don't know postmortem reports will reveal the truth."

"Deccan take him for the postmortem. I will stay here."

"Are you sure?"

"Yes. I want to know what happened to Peter suddenly I want to catch that killer."

"I think, you should take him, I will catch the killer."

"I want him alive; you leave Deccan."

"But Robin."

"That's an order." I showed my hand, that was not the time to waste. Deccan would surely kill that killer without any second thought.

"Ok sir, take care." He left with the body. Meanwhile, Emily came towards me, "How was it?"

"What?"

"My walk?"

"Yeah, that was great Emily." My thoughts are still roaming on Peter.

"What happened to you, looking stressed?" She looked around "Where is Peter and why this music has stopped?"

"Peter got murdered."

"What, but you guys were with him throughout, then how?"

"I don't know after the last performance his nose and ear started bleeding."

"He starts bleeding, how can this be possible, did anyone come near him?"

"No, we were looking at him all the time. Even when he went to clean himself, Deccan went with him to the washroom."

"Clean himself?"

"Yes, a staff member threw coffee over him as he got scared by a dog bark."

"Dog barked, when?"

"Yes, a dog barked when you were on stage and suddenly..." wait a second pets are not allowed inside and even if a stray dog cannot come in this hall, then there is no point in a dog barking inside the hall.

"What happened Robin?" I recollected all the dots.

"That staff member Emily, that staff member, we have to catch him..." If there is no chance that a dog can bark inside the hall, then it can be planned or the whole pattern of throwing coffee at Peter might be a plan.

"Staff member? Wait, Robin, where are you going, " I rushed here and there in search of that person who threw coffee on Peter. I caught the manager.

"I want to meet the staff who threw coffee on Peter." My heart was breathing heavily.

"Our staff who threw coffee on Mr Peter." His expression answered my question, "Sir maybe you got the wrong information, we have not served anything to Mr Peter as told by his assistant."

"Assistant, but Peter was all alone throughout the time we accompanied him."

"No, sir we met his assistant."

Maybe he was, "Was he look like this?" I showed him the cameraman's picture, "Yes sir he is the one."

"Damn it." It was all a plan, the set-up of the dog's barking sound was a strategy to get closer to Peter and show it like an accident.

I called Emily, "Emily, go to the security room show them our card, take the control, and play the footage of every single location, especially the exit, do check the exit of the past twenty minutes, and look out for the cameramen."

"Ok, Robin." Meanwhile, I roamed around looking for any trace of him.

"Robin, what are you doing here?"

"Anne, where were you?"

"I was following a suspicious girl we found in the dressing room."

"So did you find something?"

"No, she went to meet her boyfriend secretly, I was like seriously man, why can't you meet him directly? So, I headed back."

"But why are you looking so stressed?"

"Peter got murdered,"

"What, how, I mean what happened suddenly, you guys were with him, throughout the time, right?"

"Will talk about this at the office, now let's find the cameramen first." One thing was clear, someone was helping him, someone who knew us very well, who knew our tactics.

"Emily, did you find anything?"

"No, Robin there was not a single trace of him."

"How can it be possible, where can he go so quickly."

"Maybe he took advantage of the crowd and left after the murder."

"Possible," I looked at Anne then suddenly I collided with an old cleaner in the hall.

"Sorry, are you ok?"

"Look carefully, gentlemen." He showed his hands and moved away.

"No, Robin there is not a single clue of him, I checked out every single frame, almost every person. He is surely inside."

"But Emily, we checked almost every corner of the hall, only a few staff members are present here." Suddenly I realized that when I had interacted with the staff members earlier, I had not seen this cleaner. With doubt, I quickly turned around and asked him, "Hey you stop."

He stopped, "What?"

"Who are you, I have not seen you earlier?" I moved towards him.

"What?" He acted like he did not hear me.

"I said who are you?"

"Want to complain, go ahead." He checked his pocket and offered me his card and when I looked at it, I was surprised, it was blank.

"What is this?" I looked at him.

He stood calmly, as if nothing had happened, locking eyes with me. "my identity is written on the back," he said. I turned the note over, and there it was—"I am the killer, dear." The moment I looked up, he winked and released a rope from his backpack, launching himself onto the second floor in seconds. I fired at his leg but missed as he shattered the glass and disappeared.

I sprinted towards the exit, but by the time I got outside, he was already speeding off on his bike. Grabbing a nearby police bike, I chased after him, his speed climbing to a hundred within moments. I pushed the bike to its limits, keeping him just fifty meters ahead. Drawing my gun, I aimed, but before I could fire, he veered onto a narrow side road. I turned the same way and found him standing against me, leaning towards his bike.

"It's over now." I started my bike moving towards him. He left his bike and moved over stairs nearby.

"Not now, two more to go." He shouted.

"In your dreams." When our distance reached thirty meters, he pressed a button and his motorcycle exploded. That was horrible, I lost my balance and banged into the wall, my mind puzzled by what happened suddenly. Thankfully, the helmet saved me and I managed to gain caution after a couple of minutes. I rushed towards him, my clothes turned red, and my left leg was paining like hell, it was a blood bath, I somehow managed to hold myself and reached the terrace, pointing my gun at him, but he jumped from the fifth floor. I looked down but it was all in vain, I saw hundreds of college students practising a marathon. Where he managed to run away.

The next I remember I opened my eyes in ICU. "What happened to you Robin," Deccan was tensed, "Where were you, we tried but were unable to get a single trace of you. Thank God, Anne tracked your location and brought you here on time." Everyone was worried. But I was not in a position to talk to them. Don't know how many hours it took me to get to my senses.

I saw Anne and Deccan standing in front of me worried.

"That was all planned, the escape the marathon everything. He knew that there would be a marathon march of college students taking advantage of which he was able to escape."

"That was not the point of discussion Robin, you tried your best, don't be guilty." Anne rubbed my hand.

"Yes, brother, we will talk about it later, but for now, you have to recover." Deccan slid his hand over my head. "You are a fighter." Those words by Deccan touched my heart and made me feel worthy.

"Thank you, Deccan." I smiled at him and my eyes were looking for Emily, but she was not there, "Where is Emily?"

"She is waiting for you outside. Look, Robin, she is new to our work and when she saw you like this, she got very upset. Talk to her, she needs you."

"Let me talk to her." Deccan helped me to sit after which they both went outside. Emily entered, downhearted. Standing still looking at me in my eyes.

"What happened Emily, see I am completely fit and fine, doctors told me I will recover within a week."

She held my left leg and pressed it a little, the pain came out in my expressions.

"Fit and fine right? This is how fit and fine you are, lying to me." Her expressions and her tone broke my heart into pieces.

"Look Emily," I made her sit beside me, "This is what an agent's life is, it is not like that fancy world of richness and aura that we see in movies, it will always be life-threatening."

"I know it, I know it, I know it, you just stop now." Her anger was visible in her eyes. "I know that in this profession, our life is always at stake, but that does not mean that you go alone to catch someone, you should have told me, Anne, or Deccan for help. You work on logic right, where the hell it went that time?"

"I know Emily but at that time, it was the best I could think of off the top of my head."

"Listen, Robin, I want to be an agent, I want to catch murderers, but not at your cost, I already lost my father, but I don't want to lose you. I never trusted anyone easily, I was living my life happily, taking care of my mother and sister but now, it is not limited to them only, you..." Her tear dropped on my hand and for that moment I felt the way I felt fifteen years back with my mother.

"I love you, Robin, I love you. It is a pain to see you like this." She hugged me hard. I held her chin up, "I love you too Emily." That time I decided that although I had not promised her to not take any risk while catching someone. But yes, I will surely consider my responsibilities to her and try to avoid actions that can hurt her.

CHAPTER TEN

HE KNEW SOMETHING

Anne

The sky turned dark with the light of stars, "Deccan..." I called him out, he was walking alone on the office terrace.

"Yes, Anne." as he faced me, I saw a mix of disappointment and sadness in his eyes.

"What are you doing here?"

"Nothing Anne, just enjoying the stars." He was lying.

"Deccan," I held him, "Tell me what happened?"

"Relax Anne, I am just enjoying this view." He faked a smile at me.

"Are you worried about Robin?"

"No way, this is our work, we have to face all these injuries, I like the fact that he fought like a warrior."

"I see..." He was looking at the sky preoccupied with some thoughts.

"Then are you missing Stella?"

"Hmm..." He turned away and I got the answer, he was still missing her.

"I know that it is difficult to forget someone you love, but Deccan, it has been more than a year. You cannot ruin your life over a girl." He turned back at me.

"Anne, I think it is late enough. You should go now." His tone was authoritative.

"That would not change the reality, Deccan. It is not just about today that you came here and stood for hours. You scold Robin for being emotional, but what about you? Tell me, what is the difference? You are doing the same thing."

"I am not an emotional fool Anne, I left my home at the age when children need their parents the most, I have not talked with my family for fifteen years, but you would never understand this because you have never felt love in your life. For you, life is only about enjoying yourself, being independent, and having parties. Do you even have any goals in life?"

That was hurtful but it hardly mattered that time. He was angry and I wanted to have this conversation with him, "Okay, I admit that I like enjoying life and having fun with you guys. Now what, what about you? If you are not an emotional fool, then what are you doing now? Why can't you forget her? Why can't you go back to check on your family, your mom, who is dying to see you again? I will tell you why, Deccan—you are a coward. A coward who wants to run away from reality."

"I am not running away from reality. I am burdened by the regret that I was not there when Stella needed me the most." His eyes turned red, and I realized that in my anger, I had said too much.

"That was not your fault, you know it Deccan, our profession..."

"Our profession sucks..." He smashed his hand over a bulb and broke it, making me step back.

"This is not a profession, we are just pawns of chess that get sacrificed to clear the path of seniors, in the end, they are the ones who sweep the credit. In our profession criminals have no feelings attached to us, they are ready to kill us if they feel any threat from us." A tear dropped from his eye, "The Same thing happened with Stella."

"Threat from Stella?"

"Do you still think that the killers came for George that day?" His question froze me for a moment.

"What do you mean Deccan?"

"Those killers came to kill Stella because she got to know something that was a threat for..." He paused.

"Threat for?" I enquired.

"For many..." He controlled himself, but I wanted him to complete it. "Deccan..."

"Stella told me that she did not want to continue this agent life anymore. She wanted to leave this unsecured, threatening life and continue her passion in theatre." He took a picture out of his wallet and handed it over to me; it was Stella.

"Look at this picture, the school that you see behind is the one we had booked for Stella to teach theatre." That untold story of Stella made me emotional.

"But, how could leaving her job be a threat to someone?" I dared to continue.

"I think we have talked enough." He turned around to leave.

"Deccan..." He looked at me.

"I promise, we will catch Stella's killers."

"No, Anne, we will not catch them." He came closer. "I will burn them alive. They will experience the pain that they deserve."

"But Deccan..."

"I am not like Robin who deals with criminals logically, having mercy for these criminals will only provide them a chance to hit back."

He had left and when I heard this from Deccan somewhere I realized that his point was valid. I was able to understand why it was so difficult for him to forget about Stella. But I was eager to know what he was hiding.

"How did she die?" A voice came from my back, I turned around.

"Emily, what happened? You scared me."

"I came to call you guys. Robin has something to discuss. But I didn't want to interrupt in between, so I waited."

"Were you eavesdropping on us?"

"I am sorry but yes. Can you tell me what happened to Stella?"

"Well as much I remember, she died while saving George from some unknown criminals, who surrounded her car and fired at her till the car blasted."

"Oh, but where were you guys?"

"Robin and I were at the office; Deccan was in New York to meet his friend. Whereas Stella was dropping George at home, but it all happened in the midway."

"How did George survive?" Oh! This girl and her curious questions, just like Robin.

"Stella threw him out of the car in the midway, where he got injured also. That is all I know."

"But Anne..."

"Emily, we will talk about this in detail later. Right now, let us go see what Robin has to discuss." I skipped that conversation with Emily as I was already entangled with too many thoughts.

"Hmm, ok." She came with me but still, her mind was piled up with some thoughts.

"What happened Robin, what do you have to discuss?" He stood up holding Emily's shoulder, meanwhile, Deccan also entered.

"Deccan can you tell me what did the doctors say regarding Peter?"

"He died due to hearing a sound of more than two hundred decibels."

"What, but how, we all were there, we did not hear anything?" I asked.

"Through this." He showed a hearing aid "Someone had added a sound controller type thing in it."

"And when we all were busy in the event, he played the sound." Robin completed the sentence.

"But why couldn't Peter just throw away his hearing aid?"

"Because it was stuck with his ears and became impossible for him to remove." Deccan solved this killer's mystery. I love how he calmed himself; even after an emotional outbreak, he got back to investigation quickly.

The doorbell rang, Emily opened the door, it was a delivery man, we were expecting a message from the criminal. Without wasting much time, we again checked the box from the boom detector and opened it. This time it was George's thumb, with a message attached to it.

"Hello everyone, hope you are alive my dear Robin, I want you to be. Feeling sad for you. See I have sent you the thumb of George in reward of your efforts. Haha, Jokes apart dear, I think we should meet again, if you want George alive then bring me Jerry Rocker, that casino king, he is coming to Boston next to next week for his new Casino visit."

CHAPTER ELEVEN

ONE MISTAKE AND WE ALL DIE

Robin

"Is he mad or something, how can we kidnap Jerry Rocker? He is not just a casino king, he is a gangster, at any given moment he carries ten bodyguards, we cannot even touch him?" Anne's concern was genuine. Even I was worried about how we were going to kidnap Jerry.

"But what is the guarantee that even after kidnapping Jerry, George will be saved?" Emily did not trust the killer.

"We have no other choice. It will be our last chance to save George." Deccan's voice made a complete silence.

"Are you sure Deccan?" I know my brother is short-tempered, but I was hoping he would not commit a blunder.

"I will catch him, either with you all or alone." I was right, he had gone mad.

"Wait, Deccan, we will come with you." Anne supported Deccan, and that day I realized how blind love can be. But I could not let these guys go alone, so we all agreed to catch Jerry.

"Mr Deccan, do you have any plan or you have decided to go for the world war?" I settled down on the bed, the pain was still hurting. We all went into deep thinking.

Hours passed, I almost fell asleep then suddenly Deccan shouted, "I have an idea." He almost scared us.

"We will catch him, on the day of his visit, when he is about to check in..." It took us forty minutes to discuss and make the final plan. But it was risky, one mistake and we could die. I requested Emily to stay at the office but again love is blind, she was stubborn in her decision to be with me.

The challenge was not only to execute the plan but to execute the plan in two weeks, I tried my level best to recover as much as possible. Emily helped me a lot in this as I stayed at her home instead of mine due to mom's fear, she would panic regarding what happened to me and all sorts of things. Emily helped me focus on everything maintaining my diet, doing the normal workout, trying to walk longer distances, and following what my doctors recommended. I was successful in that, just before the day of action I was able to recover almost ninety per cent, left with some marks only.

She worked hard the whole two weeks on her systems in search of any sort of information regarding the killer. But it was very hard, the way they had hidden their identity was very difficult to crack.

"Emily, you should sleep now, it is very late, don't compromise your health." I hugged her and calmed her down I was worried because she slept on even less than four to five hours a day to crack the code.

We all entered the Casino at different times with different looks and roles, connected over call.

"Emily, what do you think, how am I looking." Like always Anne's overacting and flaunting her looks started. I wondered how she be able to collect guns from Jerry's security guards.

"Anne, be careful, you are a dancer here, don't talk with us unnecessarily and focus on your task," I suggested.

"Where are you, Emily?" I asked Emily, just to check everything is sorted.

"I am in the lounge area, serving drinks." My eyes caught her, she was looking pretty, even in that duty costume.

"Ok, and you Deccan?"

"I have entered the main hall, just playing a few games. Where are you?"

"I am here only," I became a game organizer and helped people play. Being a dealer was a tough task, spinning the wheel, distributing the cards, remembering the amount of each person, meanwhile dealing with smokers, that sucks. We all had taken our positions just waiting for Jerry to come there.

After half an hour, he came getting down from his bulletproof car with around ten guards covering him. I still don't get the idea of kidnapping him, he was the person who had committed many crimes but due to his fear not even a single report had been filed against him, according to law, we can't even touch him. I thought who would benefit from killing him?

Jerry was honoured by the manager, following which he moved towards the stage to view the dance performance.

"Anne, your turn."

"Yes," She started flawlessly, she knew how to dance well and of course acting and drama are inborn in her so she managed to perform and form an interactive connection with all of them present there. Meanwhile, Emily offered them cold drinks mixed with sleeping pills.

"Sir, your drink," Emily offered a drink to Jerry, everything was running according to plan but...

"No, I don't need anything." He refused.

"Sir, this one is made specially for you." Emily insisted.

"No, thank you, by the way, what is your name?" He asked her in an uneasy tone.

"Emily."

"Why don't you sit here and enjoy."

"No, sir, I have to do my work..." Emily dejected him politely.

"Oh, come on, no one will bother you, I pay you thrice what you earn monthly." He tried to hold her hand but she shook away. Blood ran through my veins. I wanted to grab his face and scratch his eyes for the way he was looking at her and said those words. Before the killer, he might have been killed by me.

"Sorry sir, I have to leave now." She left him and one of our plans flopped. Emily was able to deliver drinks to seven of them and now it is our time to take over. I signalled Deccan. He fired in the air.

"Everyone leave now," Deccan shouted, meanwhile I hung my gun on Jerry.

"Move a little if you want to die." His three guards and casino security came over but since I had gun pointed at him, they were useless.

"Drop your guns now, else he will die." Anne collected the guns.

I wanted to hit him hard for what he had done with Emily but his reaction "Hahahaha, you kids think that you can kidnap me?" I did not understand his laughing response, or why he was so calm.

"Are you crazy or something, stand quietly," Anne shouted.

"Before you kids do something, I want you to meet someone, bring him..." We looked at the door and five people came out of a car, holding a person by covering his face. When they came closer, I saw blood strains all over the body of that masked man.

"Who is he?" I looked at Jerry.

"Oh, Robin, you don't know him, he is Mike." At that moment I was unable to understand what was going on.

"Mike..." Deccan shouted and tried to reach Mike, but he backed off due to a gun pointed at Mike's neck. Meanwhile, Anne and I looked at each other, but she also did not know anything about him.

"What happened Deccan? You know him? Tell Robin to leave me or my guards will shoot Mike and deliver him to his sister?" Jerry threatened Deccan.

"Robin..." I never saw Deccan in that state, his eyes were red-blooded, his veins were tight, and tears were seen in his eyes.

"Leave him, Robin," Deccan uttered.

"What, but why Deccan, you know we have to take him, else George will die?"

"George, Hahaha..." Jerry laughed again, "You want George, wait..." He looked upstairs and when we turned around, we saw George coming down the stairs with a band in his hand, covering his fingers." That moment was so unexpected and confusing for me, Jerry already knew about us, Deccan knew a person called Mike, and George was safe with Jerry.

"You still don't get it, Robin? Don't worry let me make it easier for you. Put off his mask." He waved towards his guards and they removed the mask over Mike, as the mask was off, my mind blew away.

"The killer..." I remembered his face, yes, he was the killer, The Mike that Deccan knew was the killer.

"Deccan, you are also involved in all this?" The case took a new turn.

CHAPTER TWELVE

The Ultimate Showdown

Robin

I followed as Deccan said, I left Jerry and surrendered. Anne, Deccan, and I were tied to the pillars facing Jerry and George laughing at us, meanwhile, Mike, whom I didn't know how he was related to Deccan, was lying in front of George, his face was under George's foot.

"I will crush every single bone of you guys if you let anything happen to Mike." Deccan was yelling at them to leave him.

"Mr George, what is happening here, why you have tied us like this?" I asked for clarity.

"Because of your brother. He was the one who planned all these murders," George responded, his eyes burning with anger.

"Deccan..." I could hardly believe his words. "I think you are mistaken. Deccan has been the one helping us solve this case from the very beginning." I looked at Deccan, but his eyes were avoiding me.

"Oh, let me make it easy for you dear Robin, it is your right to know the truth before you die." Jerry took a sip from his drink.

"Truth?"

"George, Peter, William, and I were business friends. Our work was simple we smuggled drugs across various countries, you cannot even imagine the worth of one single transaction of those drugs, approximately thrice your salary of a month."

I was trying to understand what he was saying, but how do they manage to do all this across countries with no government interventions? I did not have any words. But Deccan's anger was at the next level, he was not in the mood to talk, he was looking into their eyes like he was about to kill them any moment.

"Tell me what you know about William?" Jerry asked me but I was listening to him quietly waiting for him to continue.

"William was not just a real estate king, but his network of brokers was amazing, he managed to provide us safest house for all our illegal activities across any country we wanted. Because of him, the Police or Government could not even imagine our work locations."

"What about Peter?" I asked like a reflex.

"Peter, my left hand, I still regret that I was not able to save him, he is the one who was brilliant at finding new clients, a great negotiator, and he supplied drugs to famous stars, singers, dancers, and sports personalities that you cannot even imagine. He helped me in managing deals in the European region while my focus was in America. His clean image acted like a shield for our work."

"Impossible, how are you guys able to fool the airport authorities, their checkpoints, how are you guys able to transport these drugs freely across countries having such severe regulations regarding all this?" Anne spoke. She just read my mind.

"What do you think Anne, how tough it can be for a person having strong connections across agents, officers, and government officials of different countries to fool them?" He laughed and I got my answer.

"George, you are involved in all this? Why?"

"What do you think I care for? I gave more than twenty years of my life to this agency and what have they given me back in return is a transfer due to the loss of one single innocent life through my revolver, that was an accident that happened in a rushed place when I encountered five criminals. I know they gave me enough money, but what about my reputation, the restrictions that they have imposed on me?"

"So, you have chosen Jerry, and you think this work makes you earn the respect that you are looking for?" Anne questioned George with anger in her tone.

"Oh, relax Anne, you guys know nothing, think practically, you guys can never touch Jerry even after running behind him, you don't know his network. Even without our support he was well off and might find new ways to transport those drugs. I supported him for a big reason."

"What reason?"

"Remember those criminals that Deccan encountered and got heavily injured for three months? What do you think, about where all those leads came from? Jerry helped us, he provided us with the leads of all small gangs, and criminals that are hidden in our location doing illegal activities."

"So, you have supported this jerk, just because of some peanuts?" I was unable to believe all that.

Meanwhile, Deccan was constantly trying to break the chain, his body started bleeding but he stretched to a level that even the pillar got scratched. The guards had to bring another chain and tie him more tightly. The question behind his reaction was still unanswered.

"You are a kid Robin; you know nothing about how things work." George interrupted.

"Why not you explain your dirty politics?" My anger boiled over as my eyes were constantly looking at Deccan, and the pain he was suffering from.

"Let me fulfil your last wish, Robin," George moved towards Deccan and continued, "You know what? One day, Stella told me that she wanted to resign soon, she wanted to follow her passion, something theatre and all. But before she resigned, she wanted to catch Jerry as she got some information about his illegal activities."

I understood where all this was heading.

George continued facing Deccan, "You know what Deccan, I tried my best to convince her to leave this case, but that blockhead, she brought about four files against Jerry with full proof about his latest drug transactions, digging deeper in which she might find out my involvement in all this, which left me no other option." He made a poker face that I wanted to punch harder. His lines were punching me, God knows what Deccan was going through at that time.

Meanwhile, Jerry faced me, with his idiotic smile, "Robin, when George told me about that girl Stella and the level of threat she became for us. I quickly created a plan, you remember George sent Deccan to New York to solve some riots, that was my idea, I created riots in New York and told him to send Deccan to lead that case. So that we can easily plan to kill that girl."

My eyes met with Deccan, and my heart went out to him. Even Anne cried her eyes out.

George Continued, "Then I appreciated Stella for her great work against Jerry and told her that we had to run quickly to my friend who heads the whole IT department of our agency and provide that information to him." He laughed, "That fool trusted me and drove me towards Willam's place, where she met Peter and Jerry. Jerry told her politely to give him that data and that he would leave her, but she was not ready to agree. I appreciate her courage; she dared to face all of us without even fear in her eyes. I tried my best, told her not to be a fool and to collaborate, even offered her millions of dollars to start her dream, but she refused."

"Not even this Deccan," Jerry looked into the eyes of Deccan, "She got out of control, she killed two of my bodyguards, smashed Peter over the table, broke his left leg when I went to her, she grabbed my neck and threw me into the wall, even when she was injured, it was hell tough to control her. But my smart boy Goerge..." He looked at Goerge and smiled.

"Finally I got a chance when she was at a call for help, I shot her from behind."

"Yaaaaaaaaaaaa..." Deccan shouted his breath out. His eyes filled with tears, and this whole scenario broke me somewhere.

"Calm down wild animal, calm down." Jerry laughed again, I wanted to break his teeth.

"She was on a call with me, only able to tell the names of you guys," Deccan raised his voice "My misfortune was that I was not there to help her when she needed it the most.

I saw George every day at the office, struggling to contain my rage and resist the urge to destroy him. Waiting for the right time, to make you feel the pain that you guys deserve, I planned all this to make this Jerry come out of his hole."

Jerry pinched a knife over Deccan's shoulder harder and harder. I was feeling angry at myself for not being able to do anything. "You think you can kill me, then go ahead, who is stopping you? See I am out of my hole."

"Deccaaaaannnnnnnn........... " My anger busted out, he looked at me, and his eyes were dried out.

"Make sure that every single bone of their body feels the agony that they deserve, have no mercy," I shouted.

"Haha, Robin," Jerry said to me, "You think you guys can do something? You cannot even touch us." He stared at Anne, "Hey, George why not, we show them a live demo. Let's kill this girl first."

He slowly moved towards Anne, but before he could touch her, the lights turned off.

"What happened someone check the lights." Jerry jerked out. Meanwhile, I observed someone break one of my hand chains, I quickly opened the other. It was no doubt, Emily, till the time light came back, all of us were free.

I quickly moved forward towards a guard and took his gun smashing him on the ground. Jerry and George were shocked. Anne and I handed the guards, meanwhile, Emily went towards Mike and hid him.

It was now only Jerry, George, and Deccan facing each other. Deccan moved his hands over their neck and dragged them on the wall. The moment they were about to die, he dropped them and smashed a table over them.

"She called me that day, she called me..." Deccan went emotional, "You guys killed her, closed that crime like nothing happened." He removed the table took them out and grabbed the collar of Jerry, "What the hell did you say, you want to kill Anne." He held Jerry's leg and dragged him over the stairs.

"You can't do anything..." Jerry was laughing like an idiot, he was unable to say clearly.

"What else did you say, we cannot touch you." Deccan grabbed his hand and with a sudden attempt broke it.

We were fighting continuously with the guards. Meanwhile, Deccan killed Jerry with his bare hands.

"What else..." Deccan lifted him and threw him on the ground.

Suddenly we heard a helicopter land over the roof, George had called the special force and they had killed the rest of the guards, now we were standing against five special cops, whom we could not fight because they were innocent and doing their work, they have no idea about the real image of George.

"Great work Deccan, you have encountered the most wanted criminal we were searching for. I will make sure you get admired from the headquarters." George started his acting in front of a special force.

I finally held Deccan's arm to calm down for a moment, we were moving outside, frustrated because we could not prove that George was also guilty and involved in all this. We had lost all hope. He could easily run away in the shed of special force.

We all came out of the casino's main gate when suddenly someone grabbed George and pulled him inside, "What are you doing?" He shouted, and as we turned around, the door slammed shut. We rushed toward it, but in an instant, the casino exploded.

CHAPTER THIRTEEN

A Gem Lost Forever?

Deccan

It took me almost ten minutes to return to my senses, "Anne are you ok, get up Anne." She was lying beside me, fine but unconscious. I rubbed her hands and sprinkled some water on her face. Then I looked for Robin and Emily, they were also fine, and the cops cared for them.

Curious about what happened suddenly, I quickly entered the main gate. As I entered the hall, I saw George lying dead inside, our revenge was complete but I wanted to know what happened. When I looked around. That was probably the third worst day of my life.

"Mike..." My sound echoed in the hall. He was lying on the floor. Covered in blood, I held him. "Why have you done this, why Mike?" Everyone entered the hall following my sound.

"We started this together, I want to end this together."

"Hey, hey champ, nothing will happen to you, I am here, I would not let anything happen to you. You remember you promised me that after we took our revenge, you would go to New York and focus on your baseball career. Wake-up champ it is time to go."

"Mike, Mike..." I repeated his name, rubbing his chest.

"Deccan..." Anne held my shoulders.

"Anne, why are you crying, nothing happened to him, he will wake up, you know he plays baseball, once you see him playing you will become his fan."

"Deccan, get up..." Robin gently held me and made me stand. Those were Mike's last words.

"We have lost him." Robin's words pinched me hard.

"Robin," He hugged me hard, "Mike endured the pain I deserve. This was the reason I never wanted him to join this mission. But his stubbornness failed me."

"By the way who was he? And why was he involved in all this?" He asked.

"He was Stella's brother and my best friend, who shifted to New York due to his father's business. He was the one who offered me to stay in his house and helped me to live in New York. His dad paid up my fees and supported me a lot. From there, I met Stella and our bond got deeper over time."

"Why have you not told me this before? Deccan..." Tears fell from his eyes, but I had no answers for him.

"Tell me why Deccan?"

"I didn't want to hurt you guys..." I answered in a low tone.

"And why not you told us about Jerry when you got all the proofs, don't you believe us?"

"I believe you guys but I knew the risk, I knew about Jerry. I never wanted Mom to lose both of us." I know Robin had a lot to talk with me, but he just hugged me, soon joined by Anne.

The stars were not shining the way they should. Even after two weeks of completing my revenge, my mind could not find the peace that I hoped for. It felt like I had fought a losing battle.

In those two weeks, I almost lost all connections with the outer environment, Robin, Anne, and Emily all tried to contact me, but I avoided them. I didn't know what to say, or how to say, I didn't want any sympathy, I wanted to live with that pain alone.

"Deccan…" That voice was familiar, but I wondered who could be there on my roof at midnight, so I turned around carefully.

"Stella, is this you?" I thought my eyes were dreaming, but she was there, I moved towards her. Tears filled my eyes.

"Look, Mike is also here." She waved her hand and I was able to see Mike, standing behind me.

"Hello, Deccan."

"Am I dreaming or something, you guys are here?" I tightly hugged Stella.

"I am sorry, I am sorry Stella, I was not there when you needed me the most."

"Don't you dare cry again," she said, wiping away my tears. "You are not the Deccan I love, tell me from when you started all this crying, whatever happened was not your fault. Don't blame yourself for what you have not done."

"But what about Mike, I would have saved him,"

"That was my decision, Deccan, not yours," Mike consoled me. "You did your best for us. You don't have to regret my death."

"Yes, Deccan," Stella added, "the battle is over now. You have taken your revenge and proven your love for me once again. Now, I want you to free yourself from the burden of the past. If you want us to be happy where we are, you need to be happy here. Make the rest of your life meaningful, help others, and go back to your family. Talk to your mother. This is the time when she needs you the most, and don't fight with Robin, always support your brother." I was quietly listening to her words.

"You forgot the crucial point, Stella." Mike looked at Stella.

"Oh yes, thank you for reminding me, Mike." She held my neck. "Deccan..."

"Yes, Stella..." My eyes were stuck on her.

"Can you do me a favour?"

"Just order, what you want?"

"If you want to see me happy then..."

"Then..." She stepped closer, I could feel her breathe.

"Move on now. Not just for the sake of saying it—move on completely."

"I...,"

"Yes, Deccan."

"I will..." I accepted.

"And remember to control your anger. Not every girl likes a guy with a hot head." She teased me, laughing.

For the first time in months, I laughed with my heart. But they were gone in the blink of my eye.

"Hope wherever you are, you stay happy," I whispered, feeling a weight lift from my heart.

I turned on my phone and, for the first time in fifteen years, dialled the number I had longed to call but never dared to.

"Hello..." I got goosebumps after hearing that voice.

"Hello, Mom. How are you?"

"Deccan..." Her voice broke into sobs. It took her a minute to gather all this, she had a million questions for me, wanting to know where I was and when she could see me. Her love had not changed an inch. She still remembered my favourite dishes. After an hour of heartfelt conversation, I assured her I would meet her tomorrow, we would have a family dinner together.

After which I dialled another crucial number. "Yes, Deccan, what happened?"

"Anne, I want to talk to you..."

CHAPTER FOURTEEN

THE LAST MOVE

Robin

We went to a luxurious restaurant owned by Deccan's friend. After fifteen long years, we are having our family dinner. The evening felt surprisingly calm, with none of us daring to touch on the past.

"Are you not eating properly, Deccan? You have lost so much weight!" Mom, being her usual self, still believed that a chubbier Deccan was a healthier one.

"Don't worry, Mom, I will try to manage my diet from now on." Deccan smiled.

"So, what are you doing now?" Dad asked in a low tone, trying to ease into a conversation with Deccan.

"I am a senior manager at a marketing consulting firm, Dad," Deccan responded.

"Just like Robin?" Dad's voice held a mix of curiosity and concern.

"Yes, Dad."

"What do they pay you?" Dad sounded concerned about Deccan.

"Let him eat in peace, will you? You can ask him more questions later," Mom interjected, a little more firmly this time.

"Alright, alright. But if you need any help, just let us know," Dad conceded, closing his 'interview' at Mom's insistence.

Mom took this chance to ask her own set of questions, steering the conversation in a different direction. "Deccan, there is something else I am curious about—don't worry, it is not about your salary. I know you are doing well."

"Yes, Mom? What do you want to know?" Deccan asked, trying to sound casual.

"What are your plans now? Do you have a girlfriend?" Mom asked with genuine curiosity, though I noticed how Deccan tensed up for a moment before responding.

"No, Mom, I am still single. I will let you know if anything happens."

"Alright then," she replied, but I could sense disappointment lingering in her eyes.

"Okay, everyone, let's focus on the food first. I don't like cold pizza," I said, trying to steer the conversation back to the meal.

With that, we all moved into light chatter. As I observed, I noticed how emotional Mom was becoming seeing Deccan after so long. She kept glancing at him, her eyes softening with every look. It was clear she was overwhelmed by the moment. Then, as if something clicked in her mind, she said, "So, from now on, no more staying alone. You are coming back with us," Mom declared, her tone leaving little room for argument.

"Oh, Mom, I wish I could. I do, but my job keeps me in New York most of the time. I will visit home whenever I am in Boston—I promise." Deccan's voice was gentle but resolute, a subtle yet polite rejection. He knew exactly what he was doing; coming home was not what he wanted.

Sensing Mom's disappointment, Dad gently placed a hand on her arm. "Don't worry, work comes first. Let him do his work," he said, trying to console her. Then he looked at Deccan with a softer expression. "Deccan, whenever you come to Boston, do visit your home."

Deccan nodded, offering a faint smile, but the moment only deepened the unspoken distance between us.

The evening eventually wound down, and as we left the restaurant, there was a moment of warmth.

"Take care." Mom hugged Deccan.

"Sure, Mom." He said and turned towards Dad, "Ok, Dad, take care."

"Proud of you," Dad said, gripping his shoulders firmly.

"Robin, are you not coming with us?"

"I will come late, Mom, need to help Deccan with packing."

"Oh, ok."

The moment they left, I noticed a flicker of sadness in Deccan's eyes that he quickly tried to hide.

"All ok Deccan?"

"Yes, let's go."

As we sat in the dimly lit car, my hands trembled as I locked the cold steel handcuffs around Deccan's wrists, securing him to his side of the door. The clinking of the metal seemed louder than it should, a harsh reminder of what I was doing. I could not bring myself to look at him, knowing the anger and disbelief in his eyes.

"What is this, Robin? Why have you locked my hand?" Deccan's voice was low, filled with disbelief.

I swallowed hard, forcing the words out. "You have had time to recover, Deccan. I did not disturb you these past two weeks, but I think it's time for you to go underground."

I could feel his gaze piercing through me, his tone growing colder. "Underground? Do you think this will solve anything? There are far more dangerous people out there, that I want to stop."

He was right—there were criminals still roaming free. And since Deccan killed Jerry, he had made plenty of enemies. It was dangerous for him to be outside, but I knew he would not understand that. After Jerry's death, his son and many others would be out for revenge. The only way I could keep Deccan from doing something reckless was to keep him locked up, at least for now. Till the time I research more on the upcoming criminals.

I finally looked up and met his gaze, though it hurt to see the frustration there. "We will catch them," I said, trying to sound firm."

"Are you serious, Robin? You think I am afraid of anyone."

"I know but, you have already broken many rules, open firing in the mall, were you crazy, you have not considered the consequences."

"You think we can ever catch these criminals by following the rules? We have to take the risks." This heavy truth weighed on my heart.

"Not at the cost of innocent lives. You are fortunate that we do not have any proof against you, so take it as a lesson," I answered.

Deccan shook his head. "I know what you are doing. You want to protect me from Jerry's people, especially his son. But trust me, I can handle it."

A pang of sorrow hit me as I looked at him. He did not fear anyone, but I could not risk it. "Sorry, Deccan," I whispered. "I don't have any other option right now. You have to come with me."

"I am sorry too, Robin," Deccan murmured, his voice laced with regret. "But I don't have another choice."

"What are you talking about?" I asked, watching as he took out his phone and quickly sent a message. A sinking feeling settled in my chest.

"What are you doing, Deccan?"

"Just wait," he replied. Moments later, my phone buzzed. It was Emily. "Yes, Emily, everything okay?" I answered, but my heart was already racing.

"Robin... where are you?" Her voice was shaky, panicked. "Someone has been shooting at the door constantly, I don't know what to do!"

The shock hit me like a wave. My mind froze.

"Emily, listen to me—stay calm. Call the security guards, grab your gun, and aim it at the door. I am coming, just hang on!" I said, my voice trembling with urgency.

"You have ten minutes to save her, Robin," Deccan cut in coldly. "You cannot reach there in less than thirty minutes."

"What...? Deccan—is this you? Have you completely lost it? Why drag her into this?"

"I didn't. I just tipped off Jerry's son that Emily was the one who killed his father."

My blood ran cold. "You realize what you have done? They will kill her!"

Deccan's expression didn't change. "You can still save her." For a moment I thought I lost her, I quickly called Anne for backup support.

"Yes, Robin, what happened?"

"Anne, quickly take a team, helicopter or whatever means, just reach Emily's house, she needs your help."

"I am there only; our team was aiming at those people."

"What, how do you..." My mind got out of the zone, too many unexpected events coming within a few minutes.

"Then shoot, what are you waiting for?" I could hear bullets in the background, which increased my tension further.

"I am waiting for Deccan's order," Anne said. "What?" I barely processed her words.

"You are working with him? Are you out of your mind?" My voice cracked with anger.

"I know what I am doing, Robin," she replied coolly. "Don't waste time—you don't have much."

I looked at Deccan "I know you are trying to scare me; you cannot do anything to her, she is innocent."

"I wish I had that control," he replied, his voice hollow. "But right now, Anne is the only one who can save Emily, and she wants to make sure that I get out of here safely. It is your call, Robin. Love makes us blind, doesn't it? She is fighting for hers too."

I grabbed his collar, fury coursing through me. "If Emily gets hurt—if anything happens to her because of your idiotic games—I swear, Deccan, I will end you here only."

"I am sorry, Robin," he whispered again. "I truly am. But I had no other choice. This was the only way."

"What do you want?"

"Just open my lock and give me the car and do not try to follow me, I promise once I cross the street, Emily will be saved." Without having many options, I agreed to Deccan's terms. I opened him up and left the car.

After ten-fifteen minutes Emily called back, "I am safe Robin, don't worry, Anne came on time."

"Thank God, you are fine, where is she now?"

"She just gave me a note and left without much word."

"Can you read it for me?"

"Dear Robin,

We both love you. It was my team firing blanks at Emily's door. We lied because we could not risk you making a mistake. Deccan knew the danger of staying out, trust me he would manage. But Jerry's son and the new gangs—they are still a threat. Emily needs you, and her safety is your priority now. We know you will not join us, fine, but please, stay out of our work. We don't want to harm you, but if forced, we will. Take care, Robin.

Your best friend, Anne"

Acknowledgements

I extend my deepest gratitude to my mentor and first reader, Dr Ankur Gangal, whose unwavering guidance, and support made completing this book possible and opened the door for me to step into the world of writing.

To my parents and my sister Vanshika, thank you for standing by me through every high and low of my life. Vanshika, your constant support, and practical wisdom have always helped me navigate challenges with ease; no problem ever feels insurmountable when you are by my side.

I am also profoundly grateful to Eshita Varshney, whose brilliant design for the cover of this book brought the story to life visually. Your patience and willingness to accommodate every detail have been invaluable, and I look forward to many more collaborations with you.

Finally, a heartfelt thanks to all my friends. While I cannot name everyone, you each hold a special place in my heart. A few of you even inspired characters like Emily and Anne, and your presence in my life has been a constant source of strength.